THE ROBOT

PAUL E. WATSON

razOr
bill

The Robot

RAZORBILL

Published by the Penguin Group
Penguin Young Readers Group
345 Hudson Street, New York, New York 10014, U.S.A
Penguin Group (USA) Inc., 375 Hudson Street, New York, New York 10014, U.S.A
Penguin Group (Canada), 90 Eglinton Avenue East, Suite 700, Toronto, Ontario,
Canada M4P 2Y3 (a division of Pearson Penguin Canada Inc.)
Penguin Books Ltd, 80 Strand, London WC2R 0RL, England
Penguin Ireland, 25 St Stephen's Green, Dublin 2, Ireland
(a division of Penguin Books Ltd)
Penguin Group (Australia), 250 Camberwell Road, Camberwell, Victoria 3124,
Australia (a division of Pearson Australia Group Pty Ltd)
Penguin Books India Pvt Ltd, 11 Community Centre, Panchsheel Park,
New Delhi–110 017, India
Penguin Group (NZ), Cnr Airborne and Rosedale Roads, Albany, Auckland 1310,
New Zealand (a division of Pearson New Zealand Ltd)
Penguin Books (South Africa) (Pty) Ltd, 24 Sturdee Avenue, Rosebank,
Johannesburg 2196, South Africa

Penguin Books Ltd, Registered Offices: 80 Strand, London WC2R 0RL, England
ISBN 978-1-59514-372-3

alloy**entertainment**
Produced by Alloy Entertainment
151 West 26th Street
New York, NY 10001

Design by Liz Dresner

Library of Congress Cataloging-in-Publication data is available

Printed in the United States of America

FOR LONG LEGGED LISA.

ALL THE BOYS USED TO TEASE HER. . . .

IF YOU'RE NOT HAVING FUN, YOU'RE DOING SOMETHING WRONG.

—GROUCHO MARX

A WARM WIND CARESSED THE FRAMES OF GABE MESSNER'S THICK glasses as he exited Roosevelt High School through the doors that led to the parking lot.

"Yo, Gabe!"

Gabe halted and squinted into the glare of the afternoon sun bouncing off dozens of windshields. The parking lot was teeming with students enjoying the first truly beautiful Friday of spring, chattering excitedly about their plans for the weekend. They were mainly sophomores and upperclassmen, as his fellow freshmen tended to be car-less.

"Over here!" Dover Mikelson called, waving his arms. He was standing next to a row of Dumpsters, in front of a . . .

Gabe nearly dropped his rock-heavy backpack. "Is that a Viper?"

"Sure is." Dover leaned back casually on the Dodge's blue-and-white hood, an easy grin spreading across his handsome face. "Fourth-gen, last of the Mohicans. You won't see any more where this came from." He patted the hood possessively.

Gabe's watery blue eyes bugged as he approached his best friend. The two had met during an enforced "quiet time" at a Montessori preschool class: Gabe was being punished for having tried to pry the keys off a laptop to see how it worked; Dover was being punished for trying to entertain Gabe by making farting noises with his armpit. Since then they'd been inseparable.

"I know your parents said you could get your learner's permit, but—"

"Ha!" Dover pushed himself off the car and reached for Gabe's backpack, unzipping it. "Are you kidding? My mom's still freaking out over the time I drove my brother's Cozy Coupe through the screened door when I was three. No way are they gonna actually buy me a car, let alone one that costs, oh, ninety Gs."

"Good point." Gabe nodded, feeling a mixture of relief and sorrow wash over him: relief because his own father refused to let him get a learner's permit until he was sixteen, and sorrow because . . . well, damn, a *Viper*!

"This probably belongs to one of the coaches who's having a midlife crisis." Dover rummaged in the backpack with one hand and gestured to the Dodge with the other. "I'm just using it as lady-bait."

Gabe shook his head. Both boys were fifteen and supersmart, but this was where they differed. Gabe was interested in figuring out computers and was especially fascinated by robotics; Dover preferred to spend his time figuring out girls. And with his tall, lanky frame, California-surfer-dude floppy hair, and hazel eyes, Dover was actually able to attract them. Unfortunately, once they entered his orbit, they were instantly repelled, either by his horrific pickup lines ("You look like my next girlfriend") or, if they hung around long enough, by his vocal love of anime porn.

"Query: What are you gonna do when the 'lady' in question finds out this sweet ride doesn't belong to you?" Gabe asked.

"I'm not worried about it." Dover zipped Gabe's pack up and bit into the candy bar he'd taken from it. "They just have to get close enough for me to ask them to party at your house this weekend."

"At *my* house? My dad will kill us!"

"Your dad won't be there," Dover pointed out through a mouthful of chocolate. "Your parents will be out of town, remember?"

Gabe snorted. "Of course I remember! This is gonna be the first time they've ever left me on my own! But knowing my dad, he'll have set up hidden cameras so he can keep tabs on us." Milton Messner was an engineer for a vacuum cleaner company called Amerivac, and he was a robotics genius. He'd once wired the backyard birdbath to deliver a mild shock to any bird larger than a cardinal. Gabe doubted he'd feel any guilt about using his skills to spy on his only son from hundreds of miles away.

"Do you think so?" Dover crumpled up the candy bar's

wrapper and tossed it over his shoulder. "Maybe we could con a bunch of chicks into playing strip poker and watch the footage after!"

Gabe sighed. "While I appreciate your resourcefulness, how, exactly, are you planning to lure an army of girls to my house?"

"Hot cars attract hot chicks. All I have to do is stand here and wait for them to come to me."

"Yeah, ri—" Gabe began.

"Hey, guys," a female voice broke in. "What's going on?"

Gabe turned to see Athena Brand slow to a halt in front of the Viper, texting on her iPhone. Athena was a sophomore, a cheerleader, and, with her enormous blue eyes and cascading waves of thick chestnut hair, possibly the hottest girl at Roosevelt High. The closest she and Gabe had ever come to speaking was last winter, when Gabe had been in line for skates at the ice rink, where she worked. He'd mentally practiced saying "Size nine, please" in a deep, manly voice for three whole minutes—but then the line had shifted, and he'd had to get his skates from Dann Murland, a sixteen-year-old freshman who ate his own ear wax.

"Uhhhh . . ." he stuttered, while Dover stared outright at her huge boobs. They jiggled slightly as she tucked her phone into the back pocket of her skintight jeans. Gabe tried to keep his gaze trained on her face.

"You're in my English class!" She pointed at Gabe with

a perfectly manicured finger. "And . . . you're in my French class." She smiled politely at Dover in a way that told Gabe she had no idea what their names were.

"*Ah, oui, mademoiselle,*" Dover said, executing a sweeping bow. "*Je m'appelle Dover Mikelson, et puis-je vous dire que vous êtes construite comme une maison de merde de brique.*"

"What did he say?" Athena turned to Gabe with a frown.

"Uh." Gabe didn't want to tell her that Dover had just said she was built like a brick outhouse. "He said he strains to emulate your pronunciation."

"'Strains to emulate'?" she echoed, giving him a funny look. "Is that a compliment?"

"Yes," Gabe assured her. "Very much so." He glared at Dover. "Your . . . your English pronunciation is really good, too," he continued, leaning on the Viper for support. "I mean, just because you grow up speaking a language doesn't mean you necessarily speak it properly, but you . . . you could be a newscaster or something—you have that flat Midwestern accent like all the anchors on Fox and CN—"

"Hey, HANDJOB! Get the hell off my car!"

Gabe rocketed off the Dodge's hood into standing position. Both boys involuntarily squared their shoulders and sucked in their breath as Macmillan Jacobs—nicknamed "Mack" for his trucklike size and his penchant for macking on any female under the age of seventy-five—approached.

"Y-your car?" Gabe stuttered, cursing inwardly as his voice

broke in a most unmasculine fashion. Athena hastily moved toward Mack.

"Now *that* makes sense," she purred, sticking out her chest and twisting her cherry-colored lips into a juicy pout.

"That's RIGHT, Tweezers." Mack ignored Athena and pushed his face up to Gabe's. "And I don't want you two turkeys dripping turkey juice all over it, understand me?"

"Sorry, man," Gabe said shakily. "We were just admiring it. Didn't know it was yours."

Mack took a step back, his angry green gaze softening as he took in the Dodge. "She *is* a beauty, isn't she?" he said dreamily, his shaggy blond hair glinting in the sun. "Look at those dive planes." He stepped past Gabe to caress the car's front, running a massive hand over the Viper's headlights lasciviously. "This bitch is so tight, it's hard to believe there's a V10 humming away under her hood, isn't it?"

Gabe could only nod. Mack had changed so much since junior high. He'd still been Macmillan then, and Gabe and Dover had occasionally gone to sleepovers at his house. The three of them had been on the debate team: Gabe could still remember watching Macmillan, cranked up on his traditional pre-debate meal of two McDonald's double cheeseburgers and a fish sandwich, delivering an impassioned argument on behalf of veganism. He had won the match, and Gabe had lost faith in the legal system.

But that had been last year. Over the summer, Mack had

gained seven inches and sixty pounds, and when he'd started high school, he'd been instantly welcomed into the in-crowd—and onto the football team. No one knew he'd been friends with Gabe and Dover. In fact, Gabe wasn't sure Mack remembered it himself.

Or maybe he did.

"What are you two douches doing tonight?" Mack asked Gabe, as Jon and Mike Nails sauntered up to join him. Jon was a senior and the varsity quarterback; plagued by cystic acne, he resembled nothing so much as a six-foot-tall meat-loaf blotched with ketchup. His brother, Mike, a junior, was a placekicker and had the kind of dark, chiseled good looks that attracted not only beautiful girls, but also their mothers. Dover had once told Gabe he'd seen Mike making out with Eva Lewin's mom in the ice cream section at Lund's. Privately, Gabe thought this might be Dover's way of telling him *he* wanted to make out with Eva Lewin's mom in the ice cream section at Lund's, but he hadn't said anything.

"Nothing special, just chilling," Gabe said, he hoped casually. "How about you? Are you going to the basketball game tomorrow?"

"Basketball?" Mack asked incredulously. Jon and Mike laughed—well, it looked like Jon was laughing. Since his mouth was like a storm drain, it was a little hard to tell. "No way." Mack shook his head. "Basketball is for pussies. And I'm planning on being too hungover to do anything tomorrow anyway. I'm having a huge bash at my place tonight." He reached out and pulled Athena close to him. She giggled and snuggled closer to him.

"Two kegs, a Jacuzzi, an indoor pool, *and* my big bro just finished building a half-pipe in the backyard. Should be epic." He looked from Gabe to Dover and back again, then clapped Gabe on the back. "How about it? Should I count you in?"

Gabe froze. Was Mack Jacobs actually asking him to *the* party of the year? In front of Athena Brand?

"Y-yeah," Gabe said. "Absolutely! Count me in!"

"Are you sure?" Mack asked.

"Definitely!" Gabe was giddy with happiness. He had never been invited to a party before!

"Okay," Mack said, as Jon and Mike sidled up on either side of Gabe, laughing. "You asked for it!"

"Wha—?" Gabe's confused question died on his lips as Jon grabbed his arms and Mike his legs.

"One!" Mack shouted as the beefy football players swung Gabe between them like a jump rope.

"Two!" Gabe's glasses flew off his face, narrowly missing Athena, who dodged them with a shriek.

"THREE!" Gabe soared skyward, arcing high and sailing toward one of the Dumpsters. The last thing he saw before plummeting behind its grimy walls was Dover, completely transfixed by the sight of his best friend being tossed unceremoniously into a garbage bin.

"Umph!" Gabe landed hard on what smelled like some musty old rolls of carpet. He lay there for a moment, blinking, wishing he could just stare at the blue sky all afternoon, or maybe sink through the Dumpster floor and be swallowed up by the earth below.

"Aaahhhh!"

Gabe rolled to the left as the sky was blotted out by a dark shape, which turned out, as it thudded heavily next to him, to be Dover. Laughter rang outside the Dumpster, followed by the thunderous sound of half a dozen fists beating on the container's metal walls. Gabe blinked up to where Mack's enormous head loomed over the Dumpster's rim.

"Ha!" Mack greeted him with a taunting middle finger. "Did you really think I was going to invite a couple of dorks like *you* to my party? Guess you're not so smart after all!" He wrinkled his nose. "Phew, somebody needs a bath!"

Gabe heard Athena giggle, and Mack's head disappeared, leaving Gabe staring at a cloud that looked suspiciously like a toilet. With a final vicious kick to the Dumpster that set Gabe's head buzzing, Mack departed, bragging loudly to his friends about all the fun they were going to have that night. Gabe sat up to try to clear the buzzing sound from his head and realized the noise was coming from his BlackBerry. It had fallen out of his pocket. He picked up the device, dusted it off, and read the lone message on its screen. It was from his father.

YOU ARE LATE!!! GET HOME RIGHT NOW OR YOU ARE GROUNDED!!!

TWO

SOMETIMES YOU MAKE THE RIGHT DECISION;
SOMETIMES YOU MAKE THE DECISION RIGHT.

—DR. PHIL MCGRAW

"HURRY UP," GABE SAID TO DOVER AS THE TWO FRIENDS MADE THEIR way painfully down Gilmore Avenue. Gabe was limping noticeably, and Dover had a bump the size of an egg on his forehead.

"Moving as fast as I can." Dover reached up to feel the lump gingerly.

"The thing I don't understand is how Mack manages to attract girl after girl. Did you see the way Athena was all over him? He acted like she wasn't even *alive*. It was like she couldn't wait for him to ignore her!" Gabe couldn't keep the bitterness from his voice.

"The Theory of One," Dover said sagely.

"'The Theory of One'? One what? Brain cell?"

"Remember when school started, and he hooked up with Tracy Ryerson?" Dover asked.

Gabe remembered all right. Tracy Ryerson was a junior with auburn hair, hazel eyes, and creamy skin. She was first-chair flute in the school band, and it was rumored that her skills in the flute department translated to other areas as well. Mack had dated her for almost three weeks at the beginning of the school year. "Yeah, so?"

"And then remember how he went out with Jenna Young, Hayley Czekaj, and Amber Logren—bang, bang, bang—right after that?"

Gabe snorted. "You mean all in a week practically? Yeah, I remember." It was kind of hard not to remember: The three of them comprised the school's synchronized dance team, otherwise known as the Bikini Board.

"The reason any of those girls went out with him is because he went out with Tracy Ryerson," Dover explained. "If girls see a guy with a hot girl, they automatically want him. They figure there's got to be some good reason she's going out with him, and then they line up. It just takes one hot girl. That's the Theory of One."

"Well," Gabe said over the hum of the Evans' lawnmower as they rounded the corner onto Twenty-eighth Street, "I'd really like the chance to test your theory out. But right now the only hot date I have is with my dad—to help him pack the car so he and my mom can get out of town and we can log onto *Halo*. You gonna help?"

"Count me in." Dover grinned sarcastically.

"Screw off."

The two boys raced up the porch steps and into the house. No one was around. They set their backpacks down near the bottom of the carpeted stairs.

"Let's go to the kitchen," Dover said. "I'm starving!"

"I think there's part of a pot roast left from last night,"

Gabe said as they made their way to the back of the house. Dover sat down at the kitchen table and began to fumble around with the ancient radio Gabe's mom insisted on keeping there. Gabe opened the refrigerator. He was moving a carton of orange juice to get to the pot roast when a loud voice sounded in his ear for the second time that day.

"GABRIEL GARCIA MESSNER!" Milton Messner barked, the words coming out in a rapid, violent burst. "YOU ARE APPROXIMATELY THIRTY-TWO MINUTES LATE! EXPLAIN YOURSELF!"

Gabe backed out of the refrigerator at top speed, bottles clanking together as he closed the door.

"Dad, I—"

"DON'T TALK BACK TO ME!" Milton yanked his head away from Gabe's ear and drew himself up to his full height of six feet four inches. He lowered his voice but kept his angry gaze fixed on his son. "You waste your time and mine when you try to explain your mistakes. Query: What is the solution to this problem?"

"D-don't make mistakes," Gabe stammered.

"That's right," his father said sternly. "Now I want . . ." He trailed off as faint digital strains of music drifted through the kitchen. "What is that noise?" The veins on Milton's neck stood out like rivers on a map. "I told you, no ringtones other than the ones that come packaged with the BlackBerry. Did you download custom ringtones after I SPECIFICALLY ASKED YOU NOT TO?"

"No, Dad, I—"

"Hi, Mr. Messner." Dover stood. "Sorry, that was just my mom texting: She said to tell you and Mrs. Messner to have a great vacation." He held up his iPhone, and Mr. Messner's features relaxed slightly. Dover's parents were high-powered lawyers who were hardly ever home. Milton Messner approved of their work ethic, which was probably the only reason he'd ever allowed Gabe to hang out with Dover in the first place.

"Hmph!" He cleared his throat. "That's very nice of her, Dover," he said grudgingly. "Please tell her we appreciate it." He looked at his watch. "We're now thirty-three point five minutes behind."

"Y-y-yes, sir," Gabe stuttered.

"I'll be glad to help pack the car, sir." Dover put in. "I, uh, missed gym class today and could really use a workout."

"You know better than to bullshit me by now," Mr. Messner said to Dover, but he was smiling. The smile faded as he looked sternly at his son. "That's Gabe's job, and he knows it. Gabe, I want you out in that driveway in three minutes."

Mr. Messner departed, closing the back door with an efficient click.

Gabe breathed a visible sigh of relief. "I can't believe they're leaving."

"It does qualify as an otherworldly event." Dover moved past Gabe to peer into the refrigerator. "Oh, *awesome*! My parents *never* buy Sunny D! Too much high-fructose corn syrup." He spun the lid and lifted the vessel to his lips.

"Wait!" Gabe cried. "That's my dad's! He drinks it after workouts."

Dover lowered the bottle. "Are you kidding me? No one else can have any of it? *You* can't have any?"

"Even my mom can't have any. It's his special treat for himself."

"Wow. That is sick and boring." Dover lifted the bottle to his mouth and took a healthy swig. Then he went to the sink, turned on the faucet, and briefly held the open container under it.

"See?" he said, briskly screwing the lid back on and placing the bottle back in the refrigerator. "He'll never know. Seriously, Gabe, you gotta fight for your right."

"*My* right? I don't even like that stuff!"

"Whatever," Dover said. "I don't know why you let your dad get away with being such a dick all the time."

"He's not a dick!" Gabe cried. "It's just . . . he's a genius, you know. He's just so preoccupied with his work, he forgets how to relate to people."

"Or forgets people entirely." Dover leaned against the refrigerator and crossed his arms. "Remember when he forgot the science fair?"

Gabe winced. He did remember. In seventh grade, he'd won first place for a robot he'd built using only found and recycled materials. As he was receiving his trophy, he'd looked out into the audience and seen his mom applauding. His dad's seat was empty.

"He didn't forget," Gabe defended his father. "He got called in to work. Besides, if it wasn't for him, I'd never have gotten into robotics, and I wouldn't have won first place at the fair. So see?" he said confidently. Dover looked doubtful.

"GABRIEL!!!" Gabe's dad yelled. "NOW!"

"Come on, Dove," Gabe pleaded. "The sooner I do this, the sooner we can log on to *Halo*."

"Gabe?" Dover said.

"Yes?"

Dover punched him in the arm, hard. "COUNT ME IN!"

———— ————

Gabe lifted what seemed like the millionth heavy black case into the back of the Messners' silver SUV while Dover offered unhelpful comments. Gabe's father had agreed to deliver a dozen minivacs to Amerivac's headquarters on his way out of town for vacation. Gabe paused briefly to mop the sweat from his forehead with the hem of his damp hunter-green tee.

"GABE! WHAT DID I TELL YOU!" Mr. Messner strode out of the family's beige split-level and across the perfectly mani-cured green lawn at the very instant Gabe took a break.

"Finish the packing in ten minutes and don't screw it up for once," Gabe repeated. As his father stepped onto the smooth blacktop of the driveway, Gabe bent down and reached for the next case.

"Oh, Gabe, Dover, there you are!"

Gabe's mom bustled up to them, towing a small, wheeled

suitcase. Gloria Messner was short and plump, with delicate features. Her dark hair wasn't much longer than Gabe's, but large gold hoops dangled from her earlobes. When Gabe had been about eleven, the earrings had been the only way to tell them apart in family photos. Looking at her now, he was silently grateful for testosterone—and puberty.

"Oh my goodness." Gloria hugged both boys tightly. "You're both growing up so fast!"

Gabe fought the urge to roll his eyes. "We just saw each other this morning, Mom, remember?"

"Oh, I know, darling," Gloria said, standing back and looking as though she might tear up. "I'm just going to miss you, that's all. My baby boy . . ." She frowned. "Dover, where did you get that lump on your forehead?"

"Well," Dover began, "you see—"

Fortunately, he was interrupted by Mr. Messner. "Query: You call that packing?" Gabe's father asked, yanking case after case out of the back of the SUV with powerful arms. "Just throwing everything in there haphazardly, thinking that'll be fine?"

"Dad—"

"Watch me, Gabe. Watch and learn. This is the proper way to pack a car." He began shoving the cases back exactly as Gabe had: in a square pattern.

"Dad, that's just how I—"

"Squares, Gabe. See how this functions? Not an inch of space unused, stable, and a slot for rearview mirror visibility."

Dover snickered. "He said 'slot.'"

This time, Gabe did roll his eyes as Milton slammed the SUV's trunk.

"Finally!" Gloria turned to Dover. "It's been ten years since Milton and I went on vacation together."

Mr. Messner dusted his hands on the sides of his razor-creased chinos. "What are the rules while we're gone, Gabe?"

Gabe shuffled his feet and looked down. "No more than one hour a day online, no junk food, no video games till homework is finished."

"Query: What is the number-one rule?"

Gabe and Dover spoke in unison: "Don't go into the lab." Mr. Messner often worked on his vacuum prototypes out of the family's basement laboratory. He was so adamant that the boys stay out of his workshop that, until they were seven, Dover and Gabe had given its door a wide berth, for fear it would be hot. One day, Gabe had pushed Dover into the door while they were wrestling, and they had been shocked to find it cool to the touch.

"That's right," Milton said. "If anyone calls the house for me—"

"His BlackBerry will be turned off for the weekend," Mrs. Messner cut him off. Mr. Messner opened his mouth to protest, but Gloria continued. "You've given those vacuum cleaners ten years," she said firmly. "You can give me two days, Milton." Gabe and Dover stared. Gloria's mouth was set, her chin raised defiantly. "You boys call me if you need anything. But remember, we're going on a retreat, and there's a reason it's called that. Any messages for your father can wait."

"Gloria—"

"Milton, the BlackBerry stays off," Gloria scolded. "Boys, call the Tsus if you get locked out." The Tsus were the Messners' next-door neighbors. Gloria gestured to the cases that filled the back of the SUV. "I'm not giving up another second of this vacation."

Gabe and Dover exchanged impressed glances. Milton's idea of a vacation was going to the Apple store and correcting the posers at the Genius Bar. The fact that Gloria had managed to wrangle him to a "love retreat" approved by her hero, Dr. Phil, was nothing short of miraculous—especially given how much Milton hated Dr. Phil. Several years ago, when the boys had been in junior high, Gloria had taken the love guru's advice about "getting back to basics in your relationship" seriously and had canceled the family's wireless Internet service. She had also confiscated Milton's BlackBerry. Mr. Messner had been furious, but she had been unrelenting, and for two weeks the family had communicated via landline. Gabe's dad had put his foot down when the landline was shut down: Evidently, even the phone company billed electronically, and so he had missed the bill and failed to pay it. Gabe remembered the two weeks rather fondly, because he *had* gotten to spend more time with his dad—and he'd been given Milton's old BlackBerry at the end. Privately, he thought Dr. Phil might be onto something.

Mr. Messner grunted and knelt to inspect the SUV's tires. Mrs. Messner ran back into the house for her purse. Across the lawn, Gabe could see Beverly Tsu doing tai chi in her front yard with her father. She wore loose pants and a pale blue wrap top that gaped dangerously in the front.

Dover was transfixed.

"Dude," he whispered to Gabe, not taking his eyes off Beverly, "she has a bumpin' rack!"

Just then, Beverly's dad, who had been balancing on one foot, spun slowly toward them and glared at Dover, his hands patting the air as though he were feeling up an elephant.

"I think he heard you," Gabe mumbled, putting his head down. Gloria swooped out of the house and grabbed Gabe in a tight hug, causing his glasses to tilt at an awkward angle.

"Good-bye, darling." Gloria released him and ruffled his hair. She blew Dover a kiss and hopped into the passenger seat, neatly avoiding Mr. Messner, who was frowning and fiddling with the GPS. Mr. Messner's lips formed a short, unprintable word, and he backed the SUV into the tree-lined street. Gloria rolled down the window to wave furiously at the boys, and Gabe's pocket buzzed. As the SUV disappeared around the corner, he pulled the BlackBerry out and read: DON'T GO INTO THE LAB!!!

THREE

ADVENTURE IS WORTHWHILE IN ITSELF.
—GROUCHO MARX

"BORED. BORED, BORED, BORED, BORED, BORED."

It was 7:23 P.M., and Gabe and Dover were lying on the living room floor playing *Halo 3*. They were slightly drunk, as they had raided the liquor cabinet and sampled everything in small measure, to be certain no one noticed. Well, almost everything: Gabe had drawn the line at a liquid with an unpronounceable name, a lot of sediment in the bottom, and a label that resembled that of a mayonnaise jar. Dover, however, had proved fearless when it came to alcohol and had downed Gabe's shot in addition to his own. Now he was kicking Gabe's butt at *Halo*, but that was only because Gabe was still distracted by flashbacks of the afternoon's events. How was he ever going to face school on Monday? How many people had witnessed his disgrace? Was he even now being referred to as "Dumpster Diver" on Twitter?

Dover unleashed his Gravity Hammer on a horde of Jackals with satisfying results. "BORED!" he said one last time. "God! What else can we do?"

Gabe moaned and flung his controller across the room. As soon as the SUV had disappeared around the corner, he and

Dover had set about doing everything they weren't supposed to do: Hence, the raided liquor cabinet and video games before dark. Dover had also searched his mom's underwear drawer. Gabe closed his eyes, but the image of his best friend holding up a silky magenta bra of undeniably D-cup proportions was permanently seared onto his retinas. Even flipping through the Victoria's Secret catalog hadn't helped erase the mental picture.

Gabe sighed and opened his eyes again. Dover was leaning close to his face, his hot breath laced with Baileys, Kahlúa, vermouth, and who knew what else.

"Do you think your parents have any porn?" he said breathlessly.

"*No*, they don't have any, perv!"

Dover crawled over to the mahogany-veneer drawers that sat below the flat-screen console. He yanked open one of the drawers and began to rummage around.

"*Seabiscuit . . . Cheaper by the Dozen . . . Mr. Holland's Opus . . .* nope," Dover said disappointedly, flicking off the television. "Let's go next door and do some tai chi with *Beaverly*."

At that, Dover was out the door. "Hey, Bea—Beverly!" Gabe heard him yell.

Sighing, he got to his feet and went outside. Dover had cornered Beverly in her driveway, where she was washing the pale-green Volkswagen Beetle her parents had given her for her sixteenth birthday. Her father, mercifully, was nowhere in sight.

"Hi, Gabe!" she said. "Dover just told me your parents are gone for the weekend. You must be really excited."

Beverly was a junior and had lived next door to Gabe since he was six and she was eight. When she first moved in, she and Gabe had actually been friends. They'd played Dungeons and Dragons together. As he got older, other boys teased him about playing with girls, but Gabe had maintained that Beverly wasn't really a girl. What girl would want to play *World of Warcraft* for six hours straight? One day, though, when he'd been nine and Beverly eleven, he'd caught a glimpse of an elastic band through the armhole of her tank top as she worked the controller frantically, trying to avoid becoming a Night Elf. After that, Gabe hung out exclusively with Dover.

"What are you guys gonna get up to?" Beverly asked. She raised an eyebrow. "Wild partying?"

"Hell, yes," Dover said to her cleavage, at exactly the same time that Gabe said, "Um, no!"

"Anyway," she continued, "if you guys aren't doing anything later, maybe you could come over for a *Lord of the Rings* marathon. Extended cut?" The invitation was directed toward both of them, but her hopeful gaze was trained on Gabe as she spoke.

"I've seen it recently," Gabe said immediately.

"Oh . . ." Beverly looked disappointed.

"But thank you," Dover broke in. "Maybe some other—"

"Come on, Dove," Gabe interrupted him, turning toward

the house. He looked back to see Dover offer a helpless shrug at Beverly before running to catch up with him. Beverly watched them for a moment, then turned back to the car.

"What is the *matter* with you?" Dover asked when he caught up.

"What? Nothing." Gabe set his hand on the front doorknob. "I saw it three times in the theater and watched it again over winter break. Besides, their television is tiny."

"Gabe, she *likes* you," Dover said as they reentered the house. "She just asked you to spend, like, twelve hours at her house. Just yesterday you were saying you couldn't remember the last time you talked to a girl!" He flopped down on the nubby maroon couch and stared at Gabe.

Gabe rolled his eyes and made for the kitchen. "Beverly's not . . . like that. She's a geek, not a girl." He opened a cupboard and took down a jar of peanut butter, then began rummaging in the pantry for some bread.

Dover shouted from the living room, "Well, she has girl-boobs! You told me you saw them!"

"I said I saw her *bra*! And that was, like, when we were kids! If she's so hot, why don't *you* go over there?" Gabe smeared peanut butter on bread, trying not to let Dover's words bother him. So what if he didn't want to watch a movie with Beverly Tsu?

Finally, Dover spoke again from the living room. "Let's break into the lab."

"Query," Gabe said, standing in the kitchen doorway with a plate of sandwiches. "What is the number-one rule?"

Dover rolled his eyes. "I *know*. But come on—you heard your mom; they haven't taken a vacation in ten years. This could be our only chance for the next decade! They're gone for the whole weekend. *He'll never know!*"

"It's just a bunch of vacuum parts."

"You and I both know there's gotta be other cool stuff down there." Dover was adamant. "Otherwise, why would your dad care if we got in? *Can* we even get in?" He eyed Gabe speculatively.

"Of course." The tiny hairs on the back of Gabe's neck rose in indignation. He might not have been self-assured about a lot of things, but when it came to his computer skills, Gabe had complete confidence. "I could disarm that thing in under three minutes if I wanted to."

"If you *wanted to*?" Dover ran his fingers through his thick, floppy blond hair, as if ready to pull it out. "If you *wanted to*? We've only wanted to get in there for, like, ever, and now you're telling me you *know* how to get in there and you DON'T WANT TO DO IT?!!"

"Of course I *want* to do it!" Gabe yelled, waving the plate of sandwiches in the air in frustration. Ever since he'd learned of the lab's existence, it had beckoned him with some kind of magnetic force. Sometimes he had *dreams* about what lay behind the door; it had infiltrated his freaking subconscious.

But staying out of the lab was his dad's number-one rule. And when it came to his father, the one thing Gabe didn't do was break rules. "I just . . . I just . . . can't. Sorry, man," he added quietly.

Dover stared at Gabe, his face suddenly serious. "Gabe, when are you going to stop being so afraid of your dad?"

The question hung in the air. Gabe glanced around the living room, where he'd spent so much of his fourteen years. There were Gloria's Hummel figurines on the coffee table. Gabe had broken one once and had been forced by Milton to replace it with months of his allowance. There was the family portrait, his mom's hand on Gabe's shoulder, his dad standing away from Gabe, like they were strangers. There were the lamps his dad had so carefully rewired to make his own version of the Clapper. He'd refused to explain his handiwork, and so Gabe had snuck down into the living room in the middle of the night and taken the lamps apart, just to understand what his dad had done. His hands had shaken the whole time, worried he wouldn't put everything back together correctly and that Milton would find out.

"I'm not afraid of him," he said slowly. "I just want him to respect me." He thought of the first time he'd used a computer. He'd been four years old, and his dad had let him sit in his lap. Gabe had immediately figured out how the mouse worked. His dad had been so proud, he'd called Gabe's grandparents right then and there, his excited voice rumbling over

Gabe's head as Gabe clicked around. Gabe sighed. That was a long time ago.

"Look at it this way," Dover said. "What do you think your dad would do in this situation?"

Gabe's left eyelid twitched slightly. He knew what Milton would do. He set the plate of sandwiches down on the kitchen counter. He was sick of being afraid.

He took a deep breath and walked across the linoleum to the basement door. He put one hand on the knob, and motioned to Dover. "Get up. We're going in."

Dover was at his side in a flash. Gabe threw the door open and jogged down the steps, his best friend close at his heels. Muttering to himself, he approached the alarm panel to the right of the lab door, next to the washing machine.

Slowly, methodically, he began to enter a sequence of numbers.

"Wow." Dover peered over his shoulder. "How are you doing this? Is it an algorithm?"

"Yeah, the algorithm of sneaking a peek," Gabe said. "I've only been watching him punch these buttons for, like, ten years."

Dover looked confused. "You told me once that it changed—that you saw him enter different numbers sometimes."

"He does, every day. But I figured it out: It's the same formula every time; it's just based on which day of the month it is. It cycles, so the code to get in on February first is one digit off from what it would be on March first. Get it?"

Dover nodded, though Gabe couldn't tell whether he understood or was just giddy with excitement.

Breathlessly, they watched as the pad's lights went dark. For a moment, neither boy moved. Then Gabe reached hesitantly for the doorknob.

"No way," said Dover, springing to life and knocking his friend's hand away. "If we're gonna get in trouble for this, we have to be able to say we *both* did it." Firmly, he turned the knob, and the door clicked open.

For a moment, Gabe felt a surge of panic, but the feeling quickly gave way to one of pride: For the first time, he'd outsmarted his dad.

"Holy crap," whispered Dover.

"Holy crap," agreed Gabe.

FOUR

TAKE CALCULATED RISKS. THAT IS QUITE DIFFERENT FROM BEING RASH.

—GEN. GEORGE PATTON

GABE'S HEART WAS POUNDING SO LOUDLY, IT WAS SETTING OFF tiny bursts of light behind his eyeballs. No, wait . . . those were the blinking green lights of . . . what?

He heard Dover fumbling around next to him, and suddenly the workspace was flooded with white light. He turned to see his best friend standing at the door, his hand still on a bank of light switches, staring wide-eyed. "Gabe . . ."

Gabe looked back to where he thought he'd seen the blinking lights. They were there all right—glowing from a turquoise-blue turn-of-the-century iMac. Other than a computer so outdated it could be in a museum, there was nothing else in the room.

Nothing at all.

"Wh-where are the vacuum cleaners?" Dover stuttered.

Gabe looked around and spotted a red-and-white vacuum standing in the corner.

"There!" he cried, relieved, pointing at the machine . . . but he dropped his finger when he realized it was the battered old Hoover his mother used for the carpet on the screened-in porch.

Dover giggled. The giggle turned into a laugh, which soon became an uncontrollable roar. Gabe glared as his friend doubled over. "What's so funny?" he asked.

"Your dad had us going . . . for, like . . . like, *our whole lives!* Don't you see how hilarious it is that there's NOTHING IN HERE BUT A COMPUTER?!" Dover mopped at his eyes.

Gabe looked around wildly. "I *don't* see how hilarious it is!" he cried, his face contorted with rage and frustration. He couldn't believe Dover had baited him into coming down here. "There's *got* to be more than this! Maybe the computer is super-special and—"

"Come on." Dover was calmer. "He probably just comes down here to play solitaire and doesn't want anyone bothering him."

"My dad isn't playing solitaire for fourteen hours straight." Gabe thought unhappily of the last all-nighter Milton had pulled. He wouldn't have spent all those hours, all those years, just avoiding his family—*would* he?

"Boy, how paranoid is your dad!" Dover broke into giggles again. He ducked into the alcove where the vacuum cleaner stood. Then the giggling stopped. "There's another door over here."

"Whaaaaat?" Waves of excitement and fear washed over Gabe at the same time.

Dover yanked at the slender silver handle. "I'm checki—"
Beeeeeeeep! Beeeeeeeeep! Beeeeeeeep!

Dover tore his hand away like he'd been burned. A loud chirping sound erupted from above, and tiny lights embedded in the ceiling began to flash white-blue light. The computer screen at the other end of the room lit up with clouds of static.

Dover ran to the computer and pressed ESCAPE, but the static raged on. Gabe moved over to where Dover had been standing. There was a tiny keypad just to the right of the door handle, flush with the wall and exactly the same color.

"ATTEMPTED CHAMBER BREACH."

Gabe stalled at the sound of the robotic voice. It was decidedly female, and despite the sweat pouring down his neck, Gabe couldn't help but notice how *sexy* the voice sounded.

"SECURITY ALERT WILL COMMENCE . . . IN . . . FIFTY-TWO SECONDS," warned the voice. Gabe gazed at the pad. The numbers one through nine were arranged in a perfect three-by-three grid.

Dover appeared at his side. "D-do you know the code?" he gasped, watching as Gabe reached out and began punching a series of numbers.

"I'm trying the same one that got us in the first—" Gabe was cut off by the sound of yet another alarm, this one similar in tone and cadence to an air horn.

"THIRTY-EIGHT . . . SECONDS."

"Aaaaaaaaahh! Try it again," Dover begged. "Maybe you did it wrong the first time."

"That's not it." Gabe scrutinized the keypad. It was in the same configuration as the keypad on the previous door: nine digits in a square, with the tenth, the zero, riding atop the center column.

"TWELVE SECONDS . . ."

Gabe briskly punched in a new set of numbers.

"THREE SECONDS . . ."

"What *is* it?" Dover was transfixed.

"TWO—"

And then, with a faint clicking sound, the pad went dark. The alarms abruptly shut off, and the flashing lights ceased. The only sound in the room besides the boys' labored breathing was the sexy robotic voice emanating from the computer.

"Welcome, Mr. Messner," it said in a pleased, slightly come-hither tone.

"How the *hell* did you figure that out?" Dover asked.

Gabe wiped his sweaty palms on his jeans. Something about the nine digits in a square had reminded Gabe of his dad rearranging the cases in the back of the van so he could see the rearview mirror.

"I thought about my dad repacking the car this morning. He kept talking about squares and how neatly they fit against each other. I just squared the code from the first pad, and then replaced the last number with the zero, which occupies essentially the same space on this keypad that the rearview mirror occupied in my dad's packing job."

Dover's jaw hung open. "Right. Of course." He was silent

for a moment. "WHAT THE HELL, MAN? YOU'RE FREAKING BRILLIANT!"

Gabe shrugged happily and reached for the handle. He turned it slowly, his heart thrashing against his rib cage. Behind him he could tell that Dover, too, was holding his breath. The door swung open smoothly, revealing only darkness. Gabe reached to the right of the door and fumbled around until he felt a bank of light switches. He flipped them up, and the room was illuminated with bright fluorescent light. As though from very far away, he heard Dover gasp.

Gabe had spent so many years fantasizing about what the lab might look like . . . and it was light-years cooler than he'd even hoped. In the center of the room stood the most gargantuan server Gabe had ever seen—it took up the whole back wall. Every surface surrounding the incredible mainframe gleamed. Vacuums of all kinds were in various states of construction; one worktable held a small army of tiny, disc-shaped vacuums similar to Roombas, but smaller and lighter. Gabe picked one up and turned it over. A bluish UVC light switched on at his touch and glowed up at him.

"Loan me your iPhone," he commanded.

"What, are you gonna call your dad and tell him we're in?" Dover handed over the device.

"No, moron. I wanna take a video, so we can leave everything exactly as we found it." Gabe pulled open drawer after drawer and found shiny parts he didn't recognize. A large centrifuge that resembled a tanning bed was situated against one wall. A computer, smaller than the one in the previous room, stood next to it. Nearby, a heap of partially assembled robotics components lay on a table, each sleeker and more aerodynamic than the next.

"Look at this!" Gabe lifted the iPhone and focused on the metal shells, pulling back to get a shot that included all three.

"Cool!" Dover came over to stand next to Gabe. Gabe reached out and gingerly lifted one of the parts up. Despite being almost two feet long, the piece was as light as a paper clip, and Gabe's arm rocketed up unexpectedly, almost knocking Dover in the face.

"Whoa!" Dover stumbled backward into the centrifuge.

"Sorry," Gabe said sheepishly, setting the piece down and turning to his friend.

But Dover was frozen, staring at something behind Gabe.

"What? What is it?"

"Turn around," Dover croaked.

Gabe's pulse thudded in his ears, his watery eyes huge behind the thick lenses of his glasses.

The centrifuge had sprung open. Bluish light spilled from the bed's hood, illuminating the hottest girl either one of them had ever seen. She had long blond hair, tanned skin, and lean, toned legs, and she was wearing a short maid's outfit. There was just one little problem.

She was dead.

FIVE

YOU GOTTA BE PRETTY DESPERATE TO MAKE IT
WITH A ROBOT.

—HOMER SIMPSON

THE GIRL'S WIDE BROWN EYES STARED UP UNSEEINGLY. GABE'S GAZE traveled up her long, slender legs to the short skirt and apron of her maid's uniform, the full curves of her breasts straining to escape the dress's low-cut neckline. He stared at her full, satiny, pink lips, at the long white-blond waves that cascaded down past her shoulders and framed her perfect oval face. She looked like she was in her twenties, but it was hard to know.

Dover swallowed thickly next to him. "Your dad had a mistress! And he killed her and left her in the basement while he went on vacation!"

Gabe gulped. As soon as the words were out of Dover's mouth, he knew they were true. But then he caught sight of something.

He moved closer to the dead girl. Had he imagined it or . . . ? There it was again—a brief point of light emanating from the girl's left eye. As he watched, the light pulsed and faded. Ten seconds later it shone again. She wasn't dead.

"She's a robot!" Gabe whirled to face Dover, whose face was drained of color. "Look!" He dragged Dover closer to the centrifuge and pointed. As Dover stared, the point of light appeared in the girl's left iris and vanished again.

"Oh . . . oh, wow," whispered Dover.

"It's incredible." Gabe couldn't believe that what he was seeing *wasn't* flesh and blood. She looked so *real*. "So that's what he's been doing down here for the last ten years. . . . Do you think he built it on his own, or is it for Amerivac? Does she just . . . clean the house?" he wondered aloud.

"Are you insane?" The muscles in Dover's neck were jumping. "Look at her! This is no vacuum! She's *clearly* a sex-droid!"

The boys stared together, taking in the strappy, spike-heel sandals the robot wore, the simple diamond studs in its ears, the pale pink ovals of its perfectly manicured fingernails. Gabe wavered. That dress *was* awfully short. But that was what maids wore, he reasoned, or at least what everybody pictured maids wearing. Maybe this was just Amerivac's marketing plan?

"There's one way to know for sure," Dover said decisively.

"Query: What might that be?" Gabe was afraid, not for the first time that day, to hear the answer.

"Her downstairs." Dover moved closer to the robot. "You know—see if she's, uh, anatomically correct. If she is, she's a sex robot. If she isn't, then you're probably right."

"That's ridiculous!" Gabe cried.

"All right, all right." Dover's voice was soothing. "Let's just look, though. Just to see."

"Okay." Gabe knew Dover wasn't going to let it go, and now he needed to know, too. "I'll lift. You look."

Cautiously, Gabe lifted her skirt. "Well?" he said to Dover.

"Oh my *God*," Dover breathed from between the robot's legs. "It's there," he said reverently.

"You mean she's not even wearing any underwear?" *Was* his dad a pervert? Or maybe he was just really, really detail-oriented. "My dad would never leave out a detail like that. You don't see Michelangelo leaving David's . . . David's *thing* off, do you? And as far as I know, he didn't carve that statue so he could have sex with it!"

Dover reached out and lifted the robot's skirt again.

"Oh . . . oh, wow," Gabe said. The two stood in silence, staring.

Finally, Dover lowered the fabric and turned to face Gabe. "You know what this means, right?"

"Uh . . . that I'm feeling really weird and embarrassed right now?"

"No!" Dover crowed. "Gabe, *we can lose our virginities to this robot!*"

"No way! I'm not letting you have *sex* with my dad's masterpiece! We shouldn't even touch it. We shouldn't even *be in here*." He looked at the robot again longingly. He was dying to know how she functioned.

"Come on," Dover begged. "No one will ever have to know."

Gabe shifted from one Puma to the other, debating. He'd taken a risk even coming down to the lab. And so far it had paid off. Who was to say when he'd ever get the chance again?

41

He retrieved the iPhone from next to the prototype casings. Moving quickly, he panned across every angle of the robot. Then he pocketed the phone and turned to Dover. "Help me get her over to the computer," he commanded. "I'm gonna figure out how she's programmed."

"I don't know if that's such a good idea," Dover said. After a moment, he reconsidered. "Unless you can program her to want to do me."

Gabe glared at him, but Dover just shrugged. Gabe sighed and leaned over the robot. Gingerly, he lifted under its arms, trying not to notice how close his hands were to its boobs. They felt soft and lifelike. He motioned Dover to get the feet, and together they carried the robot over to the worktable nearest to the computer. They gently raised it to a seated position. It slumped slightly forward.

"Hold her head," Gabe commanded Dover, who snickered.

"What's so funny?" Gabe snapped.

"You said 'head.'"

Gabe rolled his eyes. He carefully lifted the robot's thick blond hair up and scanned its jawline and the area behind her ear, looking for a seam, a tiny button, anything that would allow him entry past the skin. Gabe shook his head as he let the handful of hair fall back into place.

"Nothing," he said. "God, this thing is flawless!" Gabe surveyed the robot's peachy flesh. He *really* wanted to get into the hard drive.

"Maybe . . ." He stopped.

"What?"

"I . . . we need to bend her over."

"YES!" Dover punched the air.

"NO! I mean, I think the panel is in the back."

"In that case," Dover said, "I'll take the front."

Moving in front of the robot, he pulled her shoulders carefully forward, while Gabe reached a trembling hand toward her dress. Holding his breath, he unzipped her maid's uniform. Gabe paused. No panel. Just taut, unblemished skin, all the way down to . . . what was that?

"Hey," he said to Dover, who was very unsneakily trying to see what he could down the front of the robot's newly loosened dress. "Look at this." Reluctantly, Dover left his post and moved around to stand next to Gabe.

"Whoa, what is that?" Peeking out from the very bottom of the zipper was a tattoo made up of nine dots and open circles, in a pattern that formed a tiny square. "A tramp stamp," Dover breathed. "My mom told me she'd kill me if I ever dated a girl who had one."

"Then I guess you'll live," Gabe said. He surveyed the way the ink blended smoothly into the robot's skin. "It's the universal hacker symbol, drawn in ASCII."

"ASC-what? A butterfly would be sexier."

"It means American Standard Code for Information Interchange," Gabe explained, ignoring the butterfly comment. "I wonder . . ." Leaning forward, he pressed gently but firmly on the symbol. There was a faint clicking sound . . . and then, suddenly, a little rectangle of skin rose up, exposing smooth metal sides. Gabe carefully removed the rectangle—and then he was staring at a curving green circuit board, a web of wires, and a hard drive no bigger than the kind used to back up MP3s.

"Beautiful," he whispered.

Dover's eyes widened as he took in the sight before him. "Wow." He whistled.

Gabe reached in to remove the hard drive. The letters T.R.I.N.A. were stamped across it. "Look." Gabe held up the drive. "What do you think that stands for?"

"Tasty Robot in Need of Ass?" Dover suggested. "Turned-on, Ready, Insatiable, Naked, and Able?"

"God, will you *stop*? Can't you think of anything else?"

"Nope." Dover picked up the robot's face and ran a finger over its lips.

Gabe plugged the drive into the computer's FireWire port. On the screen, a robot icon named T.R.I.N.A. appeared in the top right corner. Gabe double-clicked the icon, and four color-coded folders popped up. It looked like an ordinary external hard drive, but the numbers at the bottom of the screen indicated it could hold roughly a million times the information. He inhaled sharply.

"What is it?" Dover asked.

"I can't believe how much is in this tiny drive." Gabe shook his head. He double-clicked the folder labeled D&V. A new window popped up with several more color-coded files. He scrolled through for a moment, stopping at a yellow one. "Here we are: I think this is where we can program her constants." Gabe noted the blank look on Dover's face. "Her personality, basically."

"How can you tell?" Dover asked.

"Well, for one thing, it's in one of the smallest compartments. There were four main folders when I opened the drive, right? We're in the Data and Variables section now. I'm guessing the biggest folder is where her motor functions are stored. You know, all the things she's programmed to do."

"Like *it?*"

"Like *vacuuming.*" Gabe glared at Dover, daring him to argue.

"Okay, okay." Dover held his palms up. "Can you reprogram her? To do things besides clean?"

"I can't exactly tell that," Gabe admitted. "But let's see." He clicked on the yellow folder. A separate window popped up asking for a password. "This stuff's locked." Gabe thought for a moment. He rapidly typed in a series of numbers, then held his breath. "Yes!" he shouted as the lock icons disappeared from the folders. "I got in the same way I got through the first door," he explained. "Only I took the letters of the acronym, assigned them each a number according to their position in the alphabet, and squared those numbers. I'm in!"

"Sweet!" Dover exclaimed.

Gabe scrolled through the file names and finally clicked on

the largest one. A text document popped up. To the untrained eye the document would have appeared to be written in gibberish, but Gabe's eyes were well trained.

He highlighted the text. "First, I'm saving the original configuration, just as I found it." He made a quick series of clicking motions, his heart beating in time with the computer mouse. What would his dad say if he discovered his son was tinkering with his one-of-a-kind creation, his Frankenstein masterpiece? Gabe gulped and focused on the computer screen, pushing ahead. He had an idea, and he wanted to see if he could bring it—*her*—to life. On-screen, he opened the Internet and logged onto Facebook.

"What are you doing?" Dover asked. "Inviting her to be your friend? Poking her?"

"I'm logging onto my profile," Gabe said. "I'm gonna download my likes and dislikes straight to her 'brain.' I want to see if I can give her my personality."

"What?" Dover yelped, as the little blue bar indicating "download in progress" appeared on the screen. "You're making my future girlfriend *you*. Put some stuff in there that I like, too!"

"I'm your best friend. In theory you like me."

"Dude. I do not want a girlfriend who LARPs."

"Okay, okay." Gabe passed Dover the mouse and shoved away from the keyboard. "Log into your account."

Dover entered his Facebook password and began typing frantically.

"What are you doing?" Gabe asked.

"I'm deleting references to foreign films I don't really like and bands that I don't care about; you know, stuff I put up so chicks would dig me." He giggled. "But now I don't have to pretend my taste is better than it is!"

Gabe rolled his eyes and took the console back when Dover was finished. He resumed loading his own profile, smiling as he took note of the I HEART ROBOTS T-shirt he wore in an old photo. While he was still in the "personality" section of the hard drive, he also programmed the robot to like video games, and then downloaded the lingerie section of the Victoria's Secret catalog to the drive. By the time he was finished, "Trina" was a hot, sexy, robotic female mixture of the two of them.

Clicking on what he assumed was the "motor function" folder, he ran quickly through its contents and surmised that the robot was capable of complex actions. He went back to the main menu . . . and noticed a folder that was still locked. *Wha?* He clicked on it. It prompted him for an additional password.

"That's weird . . ." He clicked on GET INFO; all he was able to ascertain was that it represented an extremely small portion of the hard drive. That made him feel somewhat better. "It's such a small part of the drive, it can't be anything important," he decided. "Let's boot her up!"

He carried the drive over to the robot and smoothly reinserted it into the base of her spine. Then he picked up the puzzle piece that bore the tramp stamp and carefully reattached it, marveling at the way the luminous flesh seemed to melt back into place so that the connecting seams were completely invisible. Swallowing hard, he zipped her dress back up and hoisted her slumped form back to sitting position. Again he marveled at how she looked like a real human being.

A real, *hot* human being.

"Now we just have to figure out how to turn her on," he said. Dover grinned lewdly. Gabe shook his head, but he wasn't really annoyed. Not when he was about to witness something so ridiculously cool. "Based on the configuration of the circuit board, I'm guessing . . ." Leaning around her, he gently pressed the small of her back. A tiny loading bar, barely a centimeter long, appeared in her left eye. "Yes!" Gabe cried.

"Shotgun!" Dover shouted as the loading bar began to fill.

"What? She's not a car, Dove," Gabe said absentmindedly. The loading bar was at ten percent already. *Almost there.*

"I mean first! I wanna go first." Dover hopped about in excitement.

Gabe's mouth hung open as he realized what Dover was talking about. "NO!!" he shouted. "You are not doing it with my dad's robot!"

Dover was already hurtling up the stairs. "Dibs on your bedroom!"

"What kind of pervert are you?!" Gabe yelled, chasing after him. "This is my dad's *life's work*!" At a time like this, all Dover could think about was *getting laid*?! "Would

Frankenstein knock boots with his monster? He wouldn't, even if his monster was hot!"

Dover raced into Gabe's bedroom. Gabe skidded in through the doorway to find Dover staring in dismay at the bunk bed, with its faded Transformers bedsheets.

"There's no way she's gonna go for this. Maybe we should use your parents' room." He looked concerned. "Hey, did you program her to 'feel' pleasure? 'Cuz I don't want her to be, you know, bored. I want her to—"

"Will you just STOP IT?!"

"Well, I want it to be good for her, too," Dover argued. "I—" He was interrupted by a loud noise from downstairs. "What was that?"

Both boys stood stock-still. "I . . . I thought I heard something," Dover said. "But that's not—" And then they heard the front door slam.

Together, they walked to the top of the staircase. There was no one else in the house. There wasn't even a breeze outside to blow the door closed.

"Trina?" Gabe called uselessly after her.

Dover gaped as he stared down the staircase. He turned to Gabe. "Your dad's going to kill you," he pointed out, as if the thought might not have occurred to Gabe.

Gabe's throat was completely dry. He looked at his best friend and swallowed. "Not if we get her back."

SIX

THERE IS NOTHING LIKE LOOKING, IF YOU WANT TO FIND SOMETHING. YOU CERTAINLY USUALLY FIND SOMETHING, BUT IT IS NOT ALWAYS QUITE THE SOMETHING YOU WERE AFTER.

—J. R. R. TOLKIEN

GABE ROCKETED DOWN THE STAIRS WITH DOVER HOT ON HIS heels. His dad's masterpiece was missing! His life was in shambles! His . . .

. . . mom's car was gone? Gabe stopped dead on the front stoop. Dover plowed into him from behind and nearly knocked him over.

"Dude!" Dover gasped. "Where's your mom's car?"

"NOT funny!" Gabe shouted as the boys stared at the spot where Gloria Messner's sensible, charcoal-colored Toyota Prius had been parked in the driveway. All that was left was a small oil stain.

"I thought those things were supposed to be good for the environment." Dover pointed at the stain.

"Will you STFU!?" Gabe shrieked. "Do you realize what this means? Trina—the robot—stole my mom's car!"

"What? That's crazy! I thought you programmed her to be like us. We don't have our learners' permits."

"My dad must have programmed her to be able to drive," Gabe said, awed.

"Why would he do that?" Dover frowned.

"He must have had some good reason." Gabe rose to his father's defense. "Maybe he—"

"Hey!" A girl's voice interrupted him. Both boys whirled to see Beaverly standing in her driveway. She had changed out of her workout clothes and was wearing jeans and a T-shirt with a pi symbol that slightly emphasized her breasts. Gabe stared for a moment. Dover was right—she *did* have girl-boobs.

"How come a slutty-looking maid ran out of your house and drove away in your mom's car?" she asked Gabe, crossing to the Messners' lawn. "Did you guys, like, hire a hooker or something? God, you didn't wait long after your parents left town, did you?" She laughed.

"No! No, she's . . . My parents got a maid, and she's from Serbia, so she doesn't speak much English and—"

"Your parents hired a *maid*?" Beverly stared at him. "But I thought your mom did all the housework. Is she getting a job?"

"My parents sent her over," Dover said, lifting his chin. "Since they're away and my brothers are both in college now, she doesn't have that much to clean this week, so my mom thought it would be a nice present for the Messners, since they were going out of town and all."

"Well, she sure knows how to drive." Beverly leaned against the wrought-iron railing that ran the length of the steps to the Messners' house. "I'd swear she backed out of the driveway without looking in the rearview mirror once."

"Yeah, uh, can you just stay here for a minute?" Gabe said. "We—we need to get something inside." He yanked Dover into the foyer and slammed the door.

"What are we going to *do*?" He stared at Dover. His heartbeat mirrored the BPM of a bad techno song.

"Well, you basically reprogrammed her, right?" Dover said. "Is there some way you could, I dunno, call her back?"

Gabe was doubtful. "I didn't see a remote when I was looking around to see how to boot her up. But I guess we could look again."

The two boys headed for the basement, but a quick search revealed that Gabe had been right: There was no remote.

"There's not even an access program on the server." Gabe shook his head in disbelief, his fingers flying over the keyboard. "And nothing online . . . that I can see anyway." He slammed the mouse down in frustration.

"There's one other way we could get her back." Dover looked up from the centrifuge, where he had been searching for clues.

"Query." Gabe took off his glasses and rubbed his nose where they pinched. "What might that be? Helicopter? Heat-seeking boomerang?"

"Beavle," Dover said, using the slightly rude name they had made up for Beverly's Volkswagen.

"But neither one of us knows how to drive!"

"Whatever, you were high scorer on *Street Challenger* for

seventeen weeks, remember? Driving a real car can't be any harder than that."

Gabe looked around the room at the blinking consoles, the gleaming heaps of parts, and the empty centrifuge. He had no choice.

"Okay," he said. "Let's go."

The two friends clambered back up the stairs and ran back out the front door—but Beverly was nowhere to be seen.

"Ugh," Gabe said. "She must have gotten tired of waiting and gone home."

"Oh, you think?" Dover said sarcastically. "Come on." He started across the lawn to the Tsus' house.

"What are you doing?" Gabe yelped. "We can't go over there. Mr. Tsu saw you *looking down Beverly's shirt* not three hours ago!" He shuddered inwardly. Mr. Tsu had always kind of freaked him out. He was just so frigging *calm* all the time. Gabe had seen a lot of police dramas and knew that the calm ones always turned out to be the most psychotic.

"Do you have a better idea?" Dover called over his shoulder, not breaking his stride.

"Nope." Gabe ran to catch up with Dover, who had just reached the Tsus' driveway. "But let *me* do the talking, and *please* keep your eyes above the collar line."

"What about my hands?" Dover asked as Gabe rang the bell.

"Will you—Hi, Mr. Tsu," Gabe said brightly as Beverly's father swung the door open. "Is Bea—Is Beverly home?"

Mr. Tsu smiled. "Yes, she is. Won't you come in?" Gabe and Dover stepped inside. The Tsus' house was smaller than the Messners', and the little entrance hall felt crowded with all three of them in it.

"Wait right here. I think she's in the kitchen."

Gabe and Dover looked around the living room. It was small but neat and cozy. Looking at the tiny television, Gabe realized the Tsus must have really scrimped and saved to buy Beverly the Beavle.

"We're going to have to tell her," he whispered to Dover.

"Tell her what?" Dover hissed back.

"About the robot. Otherwise why would she lend us the car?"

"We could tell her we think the maid stole something," Dover said.

"Why wouldn't we call the police?" Gabe asked. "We have to tell her."

"No way." Dover was adamant. "She'll never believe us. And even if she did, what do you think will happen if she tells her dad?"

"Ugh," Gabe said. "Here he comes."

"Beverly is upstairs getting ready for her babysitting job," said Mr. Tsu, coming back into the living room, followed by the Tsus' cat, Stockton. The cat was as fat as Mr. Tsu was lean, and its orange fur looked as though it had fallen into a deep fryer. Gabe watched in fascination as it sat down on its blubbery haunches and attempted to lick its hind foot. After a few halfhearted tries, it gave up and gazed dumbly off into space. No wonder it was so greasy.

"She's running a little behind, so she said for you to go on up." Mr. Tsu fixed Dover with an eagle eye. "Do *not* close the door behind you."

Dover swallowed, and Gabe managed a feeble "Yes, sir." Mr. Tsu stood aside, and the boys made for the stairs, stepping over Stockton, who appeared to have fallen asleep sitting up.

Gabe felt nervous as he climbed the stairs. It had been six years since he had been in Beverly's room, and he hadn't really thought of her as a girl back then. Hell, he wouldn't be thinking of her as a girl now if Dover hadn't brought up her boobs eighteen times today. He tried to focus on the task at hand. He wouldn't tell her about the robot, he decided. He'd just tell her the maid had accidentally left with something important that belonged to his dad. He'd tell her—

"Whatever you do," Dover whispered from behind him, "*don't* tell her you've never driven a car before!"

Gabe swallowed and approached the door to Beverly's room. It was partially ajar, but he couldn't see her inside. He knocked lightly.

"Beverly? It's Gabe and Dover. Can we come in?"

The door swung open fully. Beaverly stood there barefoot, in her pi T-shirt and jeans, holding a hairbrush.

"Come on in!" She put the brush down and expertly secured her long black hair into a high ponytail. "I have to leave in a few minutes, but make yourselves comfortable."

She gestured to two beanbags sitting across from each other on the floor, but Gabe stood transfixed in the doorway. The last time he'd been in Beverly's room, it had been a little girl's room, with white wicker furniture and a bed full of stuffed animals. Now there was just one stuffed animal—her favorite teddy bear. Gabe had named him Speedy, after the robot in Isaac Asimov's "Runaround." He wondered briefly if she still called him that.

Other than Speedy, the room was unrecognizable. The walls were plastered with posters from the *Lord of the Rings* movies. Mostly the posters were of Legolas, but there were several of Aragorn, and one featuring all the hobbits. A replica of Aragorn's sword, Anduril, leaned against her desk, and a pair of Elvish daggers hung crossed over the bed. He'd known she was a *LOTR* geek, but this was crazy! This was . . . actually kind of hot.

He stood there so long, he didn't realize that Beverly was staring at him.

"Hello?" she said questioningly. "Earth to Gabe."

"Uh—" Dover gave Gabe a little push from behind, and he stumbled forward and fell into one of the beanbags. "You'll have to excuse Gabe." Dover stepped smoothly in behind him. "He gets excited by the sight of men with big swords."

Beverly giggled. "Me too!" She went into her closet and came out with a pair of hot-pink slip-on Vans. "I don't know,

57

though," she said, sitting down on the edge of her bed and sliding the shoes on. "You guys definitely strike me more as the slutty-maid type."

"Actually, that's what we're here about," Gabe said, remembering his mission. "We need to ask a favor."

"Involving the maid?" Beverly frowned.

"Yeah. Well, sort of. You see, the maid accidentally left the house with a piece of equipment that's really important to my dad . . . and if I don't get it back before he gets home, he'll kill me. So I was wondering if, um, if we could borrow your car."

"She stole something from your dad?" Beverly asked, wide-eyed.

"No, no. She . . . she accidentally took something my dad built—"

"A vacuum cleaner," Dover finished.

"A vacuum cleaner." Gabe nodded. "She didn't know she wasn't supposed to use it, but it was a prototype, and he'll be insane when he finds out."

"Why don't you just call her?" Beverly leaned back on the bed's rumpled black duvet. Gabe had thought only guys had black comforters. He made a mental note to bring this up the next time he and Dover had the girl-versus-geek argument. "Or have your parents call her?" she asked Dover.

"Please." Gabe was practically begging now. He would gladly have gotten on his knees, but the dark-green pleather bean-bag seemed to be sucking him in. "This is the first time my parents have ever gone away. If we don't get it back, my dad will say it was my fault. If we call the Mikelsons, they'll want to call my parents and apologize. Then my dad will be mad that I wasn't paying attention and let her use it in the first place. They'll never leave me alone again!"

"Okay." Beverly relented and got to her feet. "I'm baby-sitting tonight, so it's not like I'd be using it anyway. You can have the car on two conditions."

"What are they?" Gabe asked eagerly.

"One, you have to have the car back by the time I get home from babysitting, which should be by ten-thirty."

Gabe nodded, barely able to restrain his excitement. They were going to get the robot back, and his dad would never know they had broken into the basement!

"And two . . ." She looked straight at Gabe, and he felt his heart stutter—with fear. *Right?* "You have to watch the full *Lord of the Rings* trilogy with me in one marathon sitting, with the lights out. Sorry, Dover," she said, smiling at Dover, who had picked up an Arwen action figure from her bureau and was furtively feeling its plastic boobs.

"No problem," Dover said promptly, setting the toy down. "He'll do it!"

Beverly paused. "Wait, you have a license, right?"

"Dover does." Gabe hoped Dover would corroborate the lie without too much embellishment. His friend just nodded.

"Great!" Beverly said. "Let me just run and grab the keys from the kitchen." She moved past the boys and ran lightly down the stairs.

"What the hell, man?" Gabe turned to Dover as soon as she was gone, struggling like a crab on its back in the depths of the beanbag. "You sold me out! I don't want to watch *Lord of the Rings* with her! Look around you!" He gestured wildly. "It's all movie stuff! She's probably never even read the books! I bet she doesn't even know there *are* books! She's just in it for Legolas and his long blond hair!"

"Well, I suggest you get into the trilogy on behalf of another hot blonde." Dover gripped his friend by the shoulders and pulled him to his feet. *"The sexy robot your dad built that ran out of your house and stole your mom's car."*

"Beverly," Gabe shouted, bolting for the stairs, "I'll bring the popcorn!"

THE CHASE IS BETTER THAN THE CATCH. —MOTÖRHEAD

MINUTES LATER, GABE AND DOVER STOOD NEXT TO THE BEAVLE. They stayed outside the car for an extra few seconds to wave to Beverly, whose client had arrived to take her to her baby-sitting gig.

"Wow, Mr. Scult looks weird." Dover slid into the passenger seat. "I almost didn't recognize him without his beard. No wonder he had one for so long—his chin is *huge!*"

"Whatever," Gabe mumbled, running his hands over the steering wheel and opening and closing the console between the front seats. "I'm just glad Beverly's not here to see me back this thing out of the driveway."

"At least it's still light out."

"Yeah, barely." Gabe fumbled with the stick protruding from the left side of the steering wheel. He found the headlights and flicked them on and off.

"Careful," Dover cautioned. "You know Mr. Ballew was in, like, World War I or whatever," he said, referring to the elderly man who lived in the house directly behind the Tsus'. "He might think you're signaling him in code and fire a round of mustard gas at us."

"He was in Korea," Gabe said, "and mustard gas has been outlawed for eighty-five years. Besides, he only keeps a BB gun for shooting squirrels."

"Well, this car isn't much bigger than a squirrel." Dover craned his neck around. "They don't call it a Bug for nothing, I guess. Ow!"

Gabe had thrown the car into gear, and the VW had lurched forward, hitting the concrete parking barrier at the rear of the driveway.

"Sorry about that," he said to Dover. "I hope Mr. Tsu isn't looking out the window." He peered at the steering wheel as he shifted into reverse. "God, this thing is ancient. I wish it had that camera that lets you see where you're going when you back up, like my mom's Prius does." He put his foot on the gas and began to back up slowly, staring openmouthed into the rearview mirror.

"God, come *on*!" Dover slapped the dashboard.

Gabe floored the pedal, and the Volkswagen rocketed backward into the street with a screech. Dover yelped as water splashed all over his lap.

"Wha—Where is this coming from?"

"Hang on!" Gabe pulled forward with another screech. The smell of burning rubber filled the car. They were on their way.

"Phew!" He glanced in the rearview mirror, where he could see Mr. Tsu, standing on his front steps, receding in the distance.

"It looks like I wet myself!" Dover wailed.

"Relax. That's the water from the bud vase."

"The what?"

"Right before they stopped making these, they put bud vases in them," Gabe said. "I think they hold, like, one flower."

"You're right." Dover leaned forward and plucked a bedraggled tulip from the floor mat. "I didn't even see it. Girls." He tossed the flower onto the dashboard and let out a frustrated sigh.

"Speaking of which," Gabe said, braking for a red light at the corner of Gilmore and Forest, "how are we going to find Trina? She's got a huge head start on us."

"Timewise, yes. But think about it: Where is she going to go? She probably went to get something to eat, so that means she's around."

"Robots don't eat," Gabe snapped as the car jerked forward again. "God, these pedals are like the opposite of the steering wheel. All I have to do is *think* about putting my foot down on one and it's like I dropped a rock on it."

"Well, you programmed Trina to be like us, right? I'm hungry," Dover said, "and maybe she thinks she is, too."

"I guess that's as good a guess as any," Gabe agreed. "Or maybe she's looking for clothes—I, for one, would be very uncomfortable running around without underwear."

"Speak for yourself," Dover said. The two friends lapsed into silence as Gabe cruised the local streets. Outside the window, the split-levels and leafy oaks gave way to scrawny young trees and ranch houses in neutral shades like white, gray, and pale yellow as they drove farther out into the suburb.

"At least I'm getting better with this stop-and-start stuff," Gabe said after a couple of minutes, shifting around as he tried to settle back into his seat. The streets were getting wider and busier as they headed out toward the mall, littered with the garish red and yellow signs of chain stores.

"Yeah, you'd have been off the road in a fireball of death by now if this were *Street Challenger*." Dover reached over to turn on the radio. He fiddled around with the knobs. "I wish I'd brought a cable so we could hook this up to my iPhone. My parents never let me play what I want in the car."

Gabe smacked his hand away from the knob.

"You need to watch the road. It's your job to look for Trina. I'm still learning how to drive, remember? What if we miss her?" *And what if my dad finds out?* Gabe felt his stomach start to tighten. He knew that if he thought about his dad any more, he might throw up.

"Take it easy," Dover retorted. "I—HEY! THERE SHE IS!" He pointed frantically, jabbing his finger against the windshield. Ahead in the distance, Gabe could just make out a charcoal-colored Prius.

"Are you sure that's her?" He glanced in the rearview mirror to see if it was safe to change lanes.

"I saw her hair," Dover said. "Her beautiful, white-gold hair. Do you think she'd whip me with it, if I asked?"

"Oh my God, she's headed for the freeway," Gabe moaned as the Prius took an angled right toward the on-ramp.

The smitten expression dropped from Dover's face as he read Gabe's mind. "We can't let her go," he said. "Just step on it. I'll help you merge."

Gabe fought the urge to close his eyes. This couldn't be happening! Steeling himself, he pressed down firmly on the accelerator. There were several cars between him and the Prius, and it was now or never.

"Okay." Dover twisted around in his seat to look behind them. "You've got the near lane."

Making a valiant attempt not to yank on the wheel too hard, Gabe eased into the left lane. *Oh my God.* This was nothing like driving on city streets. Suddenly it seemed like the car had too many mirrors, too many places for Gabe to put his eyes. He felt as though he were a lizard on an airport runway. Traffic whizzed all around him, and he felt sweat spring to his armpits. He tried not to notice the huge trucks that zoomed past him, leaving the Beavle fishtailing in their wake. Instead, he concentrated on maintaining his lane and his speed, shutting out all distractions and—

Brzzzzzzz!

Gabe nearly jumped a mile.

"What was that?" Dover gasped, taking his eyes off the

Prius, which was still zipping along several car lengths ahead of them, and looking down. "This thing has vibrating seats? What is this, the Love Bug?"

"No! It's my BlackBerry! It's set to vibrate."

"*That's* 'vibrate' on a BlackBerry?" Dover asked in disbelief. "There's no way that's standard—you could measure that on the Richter scale! I thought your dad didn't let you buy apps."

"He doesn't," Gabe admitted. "I unlocked it and boosted it myself. I guess I kind of overdid it. Damn!" He jumped as the device vibrated again. "I can't concentrate! Take it out of my pocket and shut it off. Who's calling me, anyway?"

"Good question," Dover said, "since I'm pretty much your only friend."

"Nice," Gabe snorted. He leaned forward to give Dover access to his back pocket and to give his sweat-soaked back a break from sticking to the seat. Dover yanked out the quivering device and hit "silence." Then he looked at the number on the screen.

"Shit!" he squawked. "Your dad!"

Gabe's heart stopped. "W-what?" he stuttered.

"Incoming call." Dover stared at the screen. "Milton Messner."

Oh, no. It was happening. His dad was going to find out about Trina. Gabe would be grounded for eternity . . . or at least until college. He wouldn't get to leave his room for the next three years. His mom would deliver meals on a tray, like in prison, and he'd have to play *Halo* against Dover online instead of next to him in the living room. Suddenly, steering two thousand pounds of metal down the highway at seventy miles an hour seemed like the least of his problems.

"Answer it," Gabe croaked.

"What, so he can hear you die in a fiery crash? No way. Besides, maybe he's just calling you with his butt or something. I thought your mom said he wasn't allowed to use the phone on this trip."

The phone buzzed again, and Dover dropped it to the floor. He unbuckled his seat belt and bent down to retrieve the device. Gabe swerved to avoid a Honda that he was in absolutely no danger of hitting, and Dover whacked his head on the glove compartment.

"Ow!" he bellowed, clutching the back of his skull and sitting up. He stared at the glowing screen. "It's him, all right. And it looks like we missed one—this is the third time he's called in two minutes."

"Press 'answer' and hold the phone up to my ear. He's never going to stop calling. If I don't answer, they'll come home, and we'll be grounded for the rest of our high school careers." *Or worse.* Could a person be grounded and still attend college? Gabe didn't want to think about it.

"Okay." Dover quickly buckled himself back in. "Here goes." He pressed the green button and held the BlackBerry up to Gabe's sweaty ear. A bright red Fiat full of hooting middle-aged women pulled up alongside them.

"Jailbait," the driver, a frowsy brunette in a loud, patterned blouse said disgustedly. The Fiat zoomed off.

"Hey, Dad." Gabe spoke into the phone, attempting a casual tone. "What's going on?"

"WHAT'S GOING ON?" Mr. Messner shouted. "I should ask you the same question! Why didn't you pick up the phone the other two times I called? What are you boys up to over there?"

"We . . . we're playing video games, Dad," Gabe stammered. "I finished all my homework, and it's after seven, so—"

"So you couldn't answer the phone?" Milton roared.

"I—I'm sorry, Dad. I thought . . . We thought maybe you were dialing me by accident since Mom said you weren't allowed to be on the phone."

"Your mother thinks you are to be trusted." Mr. Messner's voice crackled with barely controlled rage. "Clearly, she is wrong."

Gabe didn't bother to point out that she had evidently been wrong to trust Milton, too, since he was such a control freak he had snuck away to call Gabe.

"Did, uh, did you deliver the vacuum cleaners, Dad?" Gabe hoped to divert his father from any suspicious thoughts with talk of work. He saw a sign for a multiplex cinema zoom by. Why hadn't he and Dover just gone to the movies?

"That's none of your business," Mr. Messner said. "Now, I want you to—"

He was interrupted by the blaring horn of a semitrailer, which was attempting to pass Gabe as he drifted into the left lane. Eyes wide with fear, Gabe jerked the Bug back into the right lane as the truck, filled with squealing, oinking pigs, barreled past. Dover lurched in his seat, sending the phone banging into Gabe's teeth, but he didn't drop it.

"What was *that*?" Mr. Messner asked suspiciously.

"Uh, the video game. Dover's still playing," Gabe said hastily. He yanked the BlackBerry from his friend's hand.

"So," Gabe continued, "is the place nice? Does Mom like it?"

The only answer he received was crackling static. Then Milton Messner's voice came through in shards. ". . . abr . . . at is going on over th . . . ig trouble . . . anceled if I find out . . ."

Gabe punched the volume button on the side of the phone as far it would go, but he still couldn't make out his father's words.

"You're breaking up, Dad," Gabe said. "Are you walking around? Maybe if you try staying in one pl—"

Mr. Messner's reply came through at top volume.

"I AM STATIONARY, GABE, IT IS YOU WHO ARE BREAK-ING UP! WHAT IS GOING ON OVER THERE?"

"She's pulling off!" Dover shouted. "Quick, go right!"

"Gabriel Messner, you listen to me, I—"

"Sorry, Dad, gotta go, alien army, I'll talk to you soon!" Gabe clicked "end" and threw the phone onto the seat beside him as he pulled into the exit lane. Alongside the car, birds flew up out of the long grass. There was only one car between Gabe and the Prius now. The light at the end of the exit ramp turned yellow.

"Come on," Gabe begged under his breath as the Prius sailed through the yellow light and turned left. But the light turned red, and the car ahead of them stopped.

"Dammit!"

"No, look!" Dover said. "She's turning into the gas station." The boys stared as the Prius swooped into a truck stop and pulled up next to a pump. Trina got out. It was the first time they'd actually seen her in motion—and even from this distance, it was a beautiful sight.

"My God," Gabe said, as Trina unhooked the nozzle from the pump. She had stopped somewhere and swapped her maid outfit for a brief black slip that only barely passed for a dress. Gabe recognized it from the pages of the Victoria's Secret catalog. Had she changed clothes to be less noticeable? Smart! Gabe eyed her voluptuous form longingly as she inserted the nozzle in the Prius's gas tank. If she'd hoped to blend in, though, it wasn't working. Dover whistled. The car behind them honked impatiently, and Gabe automatically stepped on the gas, remembering to signal.

"What's our plan?" he whispered as he made for the gas station.

"This is our chance—Wait, why are we whispering?" Dover

asked in a normal tone. "This is our chance to shut her off and take her home."

Gabe pulled into a space in the side of the parking lot reserved for cars. He and Dover watched as Trina entered the gas station's convenience store. A truck driver coming out held the door for her and then forgot to close it for a moment as he stared after her.

"I'll distract her," Dover said, "and you reach down the back of her dress"—Gabe closed his eyes—"and turn her off. That's how she turned on, right, when you pressed on her tattoo?"

"Yeah." Gabe opened his eyes again. High above the parking lot, a nighthawk sounded its lonely cry. It was almost completely dark now, and the lights at the very edge of the lot flickered on with a hum as Trina exited the little store. He took a deep breath.

"Okay. Let's go." Leaving the key in the ignition to facilitate a quick getaway, he flung the driver's-side door open and stepped around to the rear of the car. Dover was just ahead of him.

"Trina!" Dover called. "Over here!"

She turned, and her whole face lit up when she saw them. Beaming radiantly, she walked toward them, her high heels clicking, her flaxen hair blowing in the breeze, her hips swaying provocatively. Her tiny, black, spaghetti-strap slip caressed the tops of her tanned thighs fluidly with every step she took, and her full breasts bounced underneath the thin silk. She was gorgeous. And she was coming their way.

"Jesus Christ!" Gabe felt a sudden constriction in his throat.

"You *did* program her to like us," Dover whispered. "But let's never forget this moment."

Gabe never did forget it—because it was at that very moment that something in Trina's beautiful face shifted. Her warm brown eyes turned to stone, and her plush pink lips curled back in a snarl, revealing bared, pearly white teeth. Gabe felt the world slow and seem to spin as she raced toward him. The spike heels of her sandals sounded like the crack of bullets against the pavement, and gravel flew up beneath them. With an unholy shriek, she leapt upon Gabe, and darkness consumed him.

RUN TO THE HILLS. RUN FOR YOUR LIVES!

—IRON MAIDEN

"AAAHHHH!" GABE YELLED AS TRINA LUNGED FOR HIM. WITH astonishing power, she brought him crashing to the ground on his back, the impact jarring his bones, making his teeth rattle, and knocking the wind out of him.

"Ufff!" Pain shot through his spine where it was slammed against the pavement. Why was Trina attacking him? She had been looking at him almost lovingly a moment before! He had always heard that girls were confusing creatures, but this was bipolar! He fought violently to wiggle out from under her, squirming until the gravel bit into his skin where his T-shirt had ridden up, but she held him down, pinning him with her weight. As Gabe struggled against her, her breasts pressed into his chest, and he panicked, using all the force he could to attempt to throw her off. Suddenly, she reared back, and he could see the night sky above them. He cringed, preparing for another hit . . .

. . . but then she reached for his hand and stood up, taking him with her.

"Come on!" Still holding his hand, she ran, pulling him toward the Beavle. Dover was already ahead of them, yanking

75

at the doors. The Beavle's back window was shattered. What—?
He heard a whistling sound and saw pavement chips flying
ahead of him. Trina grabbed him by the hair and shoved his
head down.

"Ow!" he yelled. She ignored him and pushed him into
the backseat, which was covered in shards of safety glass.
Dover launched himself in after Gabe.

"Get down!" he shouted as he landed hard on top of Gabe,
knocking Gabe's glasses to the floor.

Trina hurtled into the front seat and started the car, revers-
ing in high speed. Gabe fumbled for his glasses. Retrieving
them, he jammed them onto the bridge of his nose.

"Get off me!" he grunted, and Dover rolled off. The two
friends huddled close together. Gabe stared at the figure in
the driver's seat. Beverly was right: Trina didn't look in the
rearview mirror when she was backing up. As she peeled out
of the parking lot, Gabe hazarded a look out the shattered
back window.

A black SUV roared behind them in hot pursuit. As it
passed under the searing white glow of the halogen lights that
ringed the parking lot, Gabe made out an older, tough-looking
man in the driver's seat, and an attractive blonde woman who
looked about twenty-five beside him. *Holy shit!* he thought.
We're being followed!

"Dude!" Dover cried. "Are those the people who were shooting at us?"

"Shooting?" Gabe gazed at the constellation of tiny glass squares littering the seat and the floor and then turned to look at Trina. She was taking them onto the highway at—he peered at the odometer—ninety miles an hour. And then it hit him. Trina hadn't been attacking him—she had saved his life!

Gabe stared at Trina in the rearview mirror. She was coolly swerving around the other cars on the highway. He let his glance linger on her huge brown eyes and pillowy pink lips. This beautiful creature—this *hot babe*—had protected him.

Suddenly, he remembered something that had happened when he was seven. Beverly had pushed him down the slide too hard at the playground, and he had gone flying, landing in a crumpled heap at the bottom, a huge gash on his knee. A tearful Beverly had rushed to his side, knelt down, and kissed his wound—"to make it better," she told him. He'd gotten a weird feeling in his stomach then—and he had the same feeling now.

A loud hoot from Dover yanked him out of his reverie.

"Damn, girl knows how to drive!" Dover's eyes sparkled with excitement. Set after set of taillights flew by them and vanished into the night. Gabe peeked over the backseat again and out the hole where the window should have been. Cold air rushed into his face, making him squint. The SUV had fallen behind, but they weren't close to losing it yet. He looked at Trina again and felt a twinge of apprehension.

"Uh," he addressed her, "do you know who the people

following us are? Are they the ones who shot at us?"

Dover jumped in before she had a chance to answer. "Well, who else would have shot at us, dummy?" he said. "The gas station attendant?"

Gabe stared at his best friend. Why wasn't he worried? Why—

His thoughts were cut short by the sound of his cell phone vibrating on the front seat. He jumped involuntarily, and even Dover twitched, but Trina didn't flinch. Without taking her eyes off the road, she picked up the cell phone and handed it back to him. As her fingers touched his, Gabe felt electric sparks travel down his nerves. His heart pounded. And it pounded even faster when he looked down at the BlackBerry's screen.

"It's my dad! What am I going to tell him?"

"Tell him to go to hell." Dover plucked the BlackBerry out of Gabe's hands and flung it out the window.

"WHAT THE . . . ? WHAT ARE YOU DOING?" Shock and rage contorted Gabe's features as he stared at his best friend.

"You need to stand up to your dad," Dover said. "What's he going to do?" He motioned at the missing back window. "Kill you?"

"For your information, the answer to that question is YES! You *know* he will! And my relationship with my dad is none of your business!"

"None of my business?" Dover retorted. "You're my best

friend! I spend every day with you, and I'm sick of seeing you groveling in front of your dad!"

"Well, I'm sick of listening to you telling me what to do!" Gabe yelled.

"If I didn't tell you what to do, you wouldn't do *anything*."

"*I* wouldn't do anything? I cracked the code to get into the lab, booted Trina up, and *learned to drive* this afternoon. What have *you* done?" Gabe sneered. "Oh, right—hit on girls. Real ones *and* fake ones."

"You have to be in it to win it," Dover replied. "And if I hadn't made you do all that stuff, you'd be sitting at home waiting till the clock struck ten and you were finally allowed to play *Halo* for an hour!"

Gabe felt as though he had eaten a handful of the broken glass that was sliding around on the backseat. Dover was right. But still . . .

"Face it." Dover slumped back on the seat with the nonchalance of a winning prizefighter. "The only reason you did any of that stuff is to get attention from your dad. It's pathetic!"

"You're just jealous!" Gabe tried desperately to control his quivering lower lip. He would not cry. *He would not cry!* "You're jealous because your dad is never around for you to even *try* to get his attention!"

"Like *yours* is?" Dover looked hurt. Gabe's arrow had struck home. "Look," said Dover, "I just think you should give yourself more credit. That's all I'm saying."

79

"Oh." For a moment, Gabe felt bad that he had hurt Dover's feelings. But Dover didn't know his father the way he did—he'd never understand their relationship. And he'd thrown away his goddamn phone! Mr. Messner *was* in fact going to ground Gabe. He'd probably revoke his gaming and social network privileges, too. Gabe would spend his whole summer in complete isolation. And it was all Dover's fault!

"I'm sorry I said that about your dad," Gabe said. "But that was a *dick* move."

In the driver's seat, Trina turned around. "Yes," she agreed, looking Dover square in the eye. "It *was* a dick move."

"Aaahhhh!" Dover screamed.

"What the hell?" Gabe said. "You don't have to be such a baby about it!" He turned to Trina. "I—oh my *God!*"

A field of orange barrels loomed out of the darkness. They were everywhere—and Trina was still turned around in her seat looking at Dover.

"Turn around! TURN AROUND!" Gabe shouted. Trina glanced at him and, smiling slightly, stepped on the gas, causing the Beetle to go even faster. Gabe's heart pounded wildly. She had just stuck up for him! Why wouldn't she listen to him? Had a wire shorted out somewhere? Was she broken? Shit! They were going to die!

"Aaahhhh!" Gabe's scream mingled with Dover's.

"You know," Trina said to Dover, "you should have more respect for electronic devices."

"Okay!" Dover said breathlessly. *"Okay okay okay okay!"*

"He loves electronics!" Gabe babbled. "He sleeps with his iPhone!" Dover shot him an irate look. *What?* He was just trying to help!

Outside the orange and white cylinders began to fly by with a whistling sound. Gabe stared openmouthed. Trina was navigating the construction barrels at a hundred miles an hour . . . *without looking.* She smiled warmly at Dover and eased off the gas as they passed the last barrel. "After all," she said, "the only purpose of such a device is to help you."

She turned around. Gabe looked at Dover, who stared back helplessly. *What the hell?*

"Dude," Dover muttered, "if your dad built this chick to have sex with, he's in for a pretty messed-up relationship."

"Shut up." Gabe peered at Trina thoughtfully. "Although I have to admit, she doesn't seem much like a maid either." He cast a quick glance out of the back window. The SUV was almost a dot. But what if they ran out of gas? What if the cops stopped them? What if the people chasing them *were* cops?

"Hey," he said, trying to catch Trina's eye in the rearview mirror. "Do you know who those people are who were trying to kill us?"

"They weren't trying to kill us," said Trina. "They were attempting to stop us."

Gabe raked the gray fabric of the seat with his fingers. "How could you tell?"

"The man is six foot three," Trina explained, "and the angle of the bullets' trajectory varied between fifty-two and seventy-four degrees, which means they were aiming below the femoral artery."

Whoa, Gabe thought admiringly. At best, he'd only have been able to give a rough estimate of the angle. And he'd never have realized they weren't shooting to kill. This chick—this *robot*—was smart!

"Okay," he said, "so why do they want to stop us?"

Trina swerved to avoid a pickup truck full of teens who hooted as the Beetle sped past them, but she didn't answer Gabe's question.

He tried again. "Why did you run away from us?"

"There's something I have to do," she said vaguely.

"There is?" Gabe asked. "What is it? Maybe we can help you!"

Instead of responding, Trina crossed three lanes of traffic without looking and guided the Beetle down an exit ramp. The noise of the highway receded as the car glided down the winding stretch of concrete under a heavy canopy of trees. When they came to a stop at the bottom of the ramp, Trina caught Gabe's eye in the mirror.

"We need to find a place to hide out for a while," she said.

"A while?" Gabe croaked. "Like . . . how long?"

"Like a few hours," Trina said. "At least."

"Um . . ." Gabe looked around. There were no shops or gas

stations at this exit. A soccer field lay across the street and to the left, but its open expanses would leave them too exposed.

"I've got it!" Dover cried. "Turn right here."

"Where are we going?" Gabe asked.

"You'll find out," Dover said mysteriously. Gabe sank back in his seat, feeling relieved that they had escaped their pursuers, at least for the time being. He was glad they were going to lie low for a little bit—it would give him some time to figure out what the hell was going on. Maybe he could find out more about Trina and what she was programmed to do, what her mission was. Or maybe he could figure out what the hell he was going to tell his dad.

"Okay, make a left here," Dover said, "and then right at the light."

They were in a nice neighborhood: Large Spanish- and Tudor-style homes sat at the back of wide lawns, and huge elm trees lined the boulevard. Warm lights fashioned to look like gas lamps glimmered on the street corners.

Gabe noted the street signs as they rounded the corner: Dimmock and Frost. Ahead, he could make out the shapes of dozens of cars parked along the curb; more jammed into a driveway, and a few staked out at the bottom of the neighboring lawn. At the top of the driveway, lit by one of the security floodlights attached to the house, sat an unmistakable blue-and-white Dodge Viper.

"Dover! No!" Gabe gasped. "That's Mack's house!"

"That's right." Dover smiled broadly. "What better place to hide than a party, right? Look around." He gestured toward the hordes of students thronging the yard of the gigantic house. A couple was making out frantically under a magnolia tree that was just beginning to blossom, and a girl was puking against the side of the house while her friend held her hair. On the porch, a huge boy Gabe recognized from the wrestling team was doing a keg stand, cheered on loudly by a group of boys of similar height and girth.

"Have you forgotten about this afternoon?" Gabe asked in disbelief as Trina maneuvered the car into an impossibly tight parking spot. "I mean, I don't want to get shot either, but do you *really* think this is the best place to kill a few hours?" He gestured wildly at the drunken wrestlers surrounding the keg.

"I haven't forgotten this afternoon," Dover said, as they emerged from the Beavle and went around to the sidewalk. "But it seems as though *you've* forgotten something."

"What's that?" Gabe asked, pushing his glasses up on the bridge of his nose.

Dover pointed behind him, and Gabe turned to see the driver's-side door of the car open. A perfect foot, clad in a strappy, spike-heeled silver sandal emerged, followed by a long, tan leg . . . and then Trina gracefully unfolded herself to her full height. Closing the door behind her, she stepped into the dewy grass lining the curb and fluffed her long blond hair. She drew a tiny tube of gloss from her pocket and ran it over her lush pink lips. Pouting, she replaced the lip gloss. Then she held out a hand to each boy.

As they took her surprisingly warm hands in their sweaty ones, Dover leaned around and grinned at Gabe.

"You forgot the Theory of One."

CIVILIZATION IS UNBEARABLE, BUT IT IS LESS
UNBEARABLE AT THE TOP.   —TIMOTHY LEARY

DOVER WAS RIGHT ABOUT TWO THINGS: GABE *HAD* FORGOTTEN about the Theory of One. And the Theory of One . . . worked.

As the trio crossed the front lawn, the wrestlers on the porch stopped cheering and stared, their eyes lewdly raking Trina's form from top to bottom. Gabe was suddenly overwhelmed with the desire to fight every one of them. He knew, however, that he'd be rendered toothless within the first three seconds of such an altercation. The girl who'd been holding her friend's hair as she puked loosened her grip, causing the barfing girl to stumble blindly against the house. And the couple who'd been making out so passionately a moment ago broke apart, as the boy appeared to forget that he wasn't alone, his eyes widening and his lips going slack. The angry slap he received across the face appeared to have little effect. He continued to stare after Trina while raising one hand absentmindedly to his reddening cheek. Gabe had to work hard to keep his own mouth shut as everyone else's fell open.

When they reached the porch, Trina dropped Gabe and Dover's hands with a squeeze, and the three climbed the steps in silence. Gabe's palms grew even sweatier. Should he say something? What if everyone had heard about what had happened this afternoon with Mack? Would the wrestler from school recognize them and tell Mack they were there?

The thoughts swirling in his head dissipated as Trina spoke.

"Gosh, I'm thirsty," she said in a voice that managed to be alluring yet innocent at the same time.

"Uh, do you want a beer?" The boy who had been doing the keg stand practically tripped over his friends in his attempt to offer her a huge, bright-red plastic cup sloshing with foam.

Trina flashed a heart-melting smile at him. "That is so sweet, but I'm afraid it's a little early for me to start drinking. I'm a bit of a lightweight." She giggled as the boy's eyes widened. "Gabe, darling," she cooed, turning to him and reaching up to touch his chest, "do you think you could take me inside to get something more . . . virgin?"

Holy. Shit. Gabe locked eyes with the wrestler. At that moment, he realized that the enormous boy didn't recognize him. He realized something else: The guy was impressed. Nodding slightly to Gabe, the wrestler backed away, almost stepping on his friends' feet as he loudly resumed whatever conversation they'd been having. Gabe, remembering every *Bourne* movie he'd ever seen, placed his hand lightly on the small of Trina's back. Being careful not to press too hard lest he power her down, he guided her through the door of the house, with Dover close on their heels.

If Gabe had thought the scene outside was crazy, the one that greeted them inside was total bedlam. Kids were everywhere, dancing on the coffee table, draped over furniture, yanking books from their shelves, grinding cigarettes and mud into the carpet. Couch pillows flew through the air. Occasionally, one knocked a few crystals from a partially denuded crystal chandelier that hung at an increasingly treacherous angle from the ceiling. Two boys in a corner made matching O-faces as they DJ'ed. The music blasted from several sets of mismatched speakers that appeared to have been ripped from their moorings and scattered haphazardly through the living room. Gabe spied one lying sideways in a mechanical baby swing. He wondered briefly where the contraption's original occupant was.

Just beyond the swing, a wide archway led into an elegant dining room. Two boys with short Mohawks held a pair of fishnet stockings stretched low over a polished mahogany table, forming a net, while their dates played strip Ping-Pong. The girls were using plates as paddles.

"Oooops!" one of the girls shrieked as her plate shattered on the floor. Behind her, a china cabinet gaped open. She reached into it and took out a thin white plate with gold edges. "Your serve!" she yelled. Then she passed out face-first on the table. "Stephaniieeeeeee!" the other girl came around to tug at the bra biting into her friend's back. "You lose!! Take it oooooffffffff!!"

"Wow, I don't even recognize any of these people," Gabe called to Dover.

"Me neither."

"They must go to Lincoln or North," Gabe shouted,

referring to two of the city's other high schools.

"It looks like there are *college girls* here!" Dover pointed to a group of girls in tiny cutoff shorts clustered around a couch. As Gabe watched, a stunning blonde in a sleeveless red-and-black Texas Tech T-shirt lay down on the back of the couch. She pulled up her shirt, revealing a toned midriff. A black-haired girl with huge boobs spilling out of a hot-pink bikini top approached her, holding a shot glass. Giggling, she emptied the contents of the cup onto the blonde's stomach. Her friends hooted and shrieked as the brunette bent to lap up the liquid.

"Body shots!" Dover hooted. "Sa-weet! Man, I hope there are some chicks here from L'École, too!" he said, citing the private French academy that was just a few blocks away from Roosevelt. "Those French babes are *hot*!"

Gabe couldn't believe he cared about any of them. He squeezed Trina's hand. She was beyond a shadow of a doubt the most beautiful girl at the party. *Only*, he reminded himself ruefully, *she isn't a girl.*

"Want a shot?" One of the college girls had abandoned her friends and was standing unsteadily in front of him, holding a small, clear-plastic cup of green Jell-O. It quivered slightly in the girl's fist. Her taut stomach was wet from where her hot friends had been licking it. Gabe tried to pull his gaze up but found himself staring into her swelling cleavage instead. He could see the tiny flower that decorated the front of her bra, right where it plunged between her—

"Hell yes!" Dover swooped in and grabbed the cup out of the girl's hand. "Can I lick it off your stomach?"

"No way!" the girl said. Dover looked disappointed. "It's Melanie's turn!" she squealed, dragging him over to the couch, where a pretty redhead greeted him warmly before stretching out obligingly and pulling her thin, white T-shirt up and over her bra. Gabe stared as Dover dumped the shot into her belly button and slurped it up like a pro.

"It's vodka!" he shouted. "Gabe, you gotta try this!"

"Uh, I think . . . I think I'll pass," Gabe said as the first girl bore down on him and Trina with a tray of shots and a maniacal giggle.

"Good idea," a rich, masculine voice broke in. Gabe turned to see Troy Hernandez, widely hailed by girls at Roosevelt as the handsomest freshman boy in school, standing behind him. Troy was president of their class and such a good swimmer and tennis player that he had made both the varsity teams despite his freshman status. Now he leaned in to whisper conspiratorially to Gabe, his plain white T-shirt accentuating his tanned, muscular arms. Gabe could practically hear his abs rippling underneath the soft fabric.

"Don't even bother with these chicks," he said in a low tone. Gabe stiffened, ready for a fight. But Troy continued. "I don't know why they think they have a chance when you're with *her*." He indicated Trina, who was politely holding a Jell-O shot and looking around.

Gabe relaxed. He was about to thank Troy and tell him he was no slouch himself in the attracting-hot-chicks department when Troy spoke again. "What school do you go to?" he asked. "Lincoln?"

"Um . . ." Gabe found himself at a loss for words as he looked into Troy's earnest, handsome face. He had gone to school with him since he was five. Sure, they didn't have any classes together, but come *on*! Troy's locker was across the hall from his! "I go to Roosevelt," he said, trying to keep the indignation from his voice.

"Wow, just started, huh? Well, welcome!" Troy shook his hand warmly. "Listen, let me give you and . . . what did you say your girlfriend's name was?"

"Trina." Gabe felt a jolt of pleasure at hearing her referred to as his girlfriend.

"Yes, Gabe?" Her breasts jiggled as she set down her Jell-O shot. Troy stared and Gabe smirked back at him, feeling his confidence rise.

"Let me give you and Trina a tour of the house," Troy said. "Unless you've been here before? You know Mack, right?"

"Yeah." Gabe decided it would be best to keep his answer as short as possible. "I haven't been here before."

"Well," Troy clapped him on the shoulder, "you'll definitely be chilling here a lot from now on, so check it out!"

He led Gabe and Trina through the bottom of the massive house. Dover followed, with Melanie and two of the other college girls clinging to him. His eyes were bright with happiness.

Gabe hadn't known a house could have so many rooms.

"A friggin' *art gallery*?" he muttered to Dover as they passed through a huge white room that held nothing but enormous, smeary canvases and a sculpture that looked like a giant, disembodied anus. Several sophomore boys were huddled around it, arguing about how to smoke pot out of it.

Dover shrugged. "I read somewhere it's a good investment. Yo! My man!" he yelled to Troy, who had moved ahead a few steps. Troy turned around.

"'Sup?"

"Isn't there a pool around here somewhere?" Dover asked.

"Hell, yeah, there is." Troy grinned broadly. "And it's indoors, so we can rage all night long without the neighbors complaining!" Gabe cast an eye toward a nearby window. The backyard was a seething mass of screaming teenagers. If the neighbors hadn't complained by now, they never would.

Troy led the group down a short, glass-walled breezeway toward the sound of booming hip-hop. "Since you're new to Roosevelt," he called over his shoulder, "you probably don't know about our school tradition." Gabe cast a quick glance at Dover to see if he'd heard Troy, but Dover was attempting to nibble Melanie's earlobe.

"What tradition is that?" The music grew louder as they drew closer to the end of the hall, and Gabe could feel his rib cage vibrating.

"Coed water polo!" Troy shouted, as they stepped out of the

breezeway and into a huge, glass-walled solarium. A vast pool stretched out in front of them. At least a hundred kids were in the pool, shrieking and shouting. The pool was painted black, and huge lights studded the walls below the water, illuminating the polo players. Gabe squinted. Was that girl *naked*?

"How come it's all doubles?" There were almost no single players. Mostly, girls rode around on boys' shoulders, but he saw a couple of girl-girl couples as well. He swallowed thickly.

"We're the Roosevelt Roughriders," Troy explained, as if Gabe didn't know. "So this is how we roll. You get to be the horse or you get to be the rider." He winked. "Saddle up!"

The game surged toward their end of the pool, and two girls launched themselves at the ball at once. They collided, and sent a tremendous plume of water toward the breezeway entrance. Trina gave a little gasp and jumped back. The water splatted harmlessly at their feet.

Oh, no! Gabe thought. *What if she gets wet? Will she short out? Is her skin waterproof?* Surely his dad had thought of that, right? He was distracted from these thoughts as the ball whizzed by his head. Trina caught it, a little too swiftly. Gabe froze, but no one seemed to notice.

"Come on in!" Dina Berstein shouted. She was a freshman who had previously paid him the same amount of attention girls generally paid to classroom announcements, whole-milk lattes, and the sale rack at Hot Topic—which is to say, none. She rose dripping from the water in her turquoise bikini, her long, honey-colored hair clinging to her skin, and waved her hands over her head. Britney Lewin, Eva Lewin's big sister, swam over. She had recently cut her dark hair short and looked tough and sexy in a camouflage string bikini. She grabbed Dina and pulled her back into the water. The two girls shrieked and splashed each other.

Dover didn't have to be asked twice. He tore off his Busted T-shirt, grabbed the ball from Trina, and cannonballed past Gabe. He landed in the pool with an enormous splash. The college girls dove in after him, still in their cutoff shorts. Gabe was torn between his desire to play water polo with his bikini-clad classmates and his concern for Trina. She didn't seem to mind the splashes, but he was pretty sure she couldn't take complete immersion in the pool. And he certainly wasn't going to leave her out here with the hordes of junior boys gawking from the diving board.

Fortunately, Troy read his hesitancy as disdain.

"Yeah, can't say I blame you," he said. "I spend enough time in the pool as it is." He motioned to the wet bar that stood at the back of the room. "Let's go have a decent drink while the kids play around. Do you drink martinis?"

The closest Gabe had ever come to a martini was seeing a giant picture of one on the side of a bus, but he wasn't about to let Troy know that.

"Yeah, sure. Extra-dry, please." He wasn't sure what that meant, but he had heard it somewhere—maybe in an old James Bond movie—and it sounded cool.

"You got it!" They headed to the bar, where Troy was greeted by several other boys wearing swim team shirts from various local high schools, and a couple of Roosevelt sophomore cheerleaders. Troy introduced Gabe and Trina around and set about mixing the drinks.

"How are you doing?" Gabe asked Trina softly. Robot or not, it was his first time at a real party with a girl. Even though they were on the run, he wanted her to have a good time. But he still felt awkward making conversation.

"I'm having fun." Trina smiled. "I think I might go play water polo."

"What?" Gabe asked. "Won't you . . . won't you short out?" Then he froze. Did she *know* she was a robot? What if the question threw her into an existential crisis? His ears burned. Why couldn't he have just offered her a beer?

"No." She squeezed his hand. "Anything you can do, I can do. I was just kidding about the water polo, though." She craned her swanlike neck. "But I do need to find a bathroom."

Gabe blinked. Why would a robot need a bathroom? He couldn't bring himself to ask her.

"Uh, there's one by the breezeway entrance," he said, trying not to blush. He pointed to the other side of the pool.

Trina gave his hand another squeeze. "I'll be back in five minutes."

Gabe watched her click daintily away, taking the eyes of every boy in the room with her. She managed to reach the bathroom unmolested and closed the door behind her. Gabe finally began to relax. There was just one thing that was bothering him.

"Where's Mack?" he asked Troy. "I haven't seen him all night."

A dark-haired boy wearing a Speedo sniggered.

"He's upstairs juggling some girl's jubblies," the boy said. "That's the third one he's had up there tonight!"

"Yeah, but who's counting?" whooped a boy with white-blond hair and a lopsided grin.

"Mike and Jon, probably." Gabe felt brave. "On their fingers!"

The blond boy laughed and offered his hand for a high five. Troy, grinning, shoved a sloshing martini glass in his other hand. Gabe sipped it gingerly. It tasted like shit but burned pleasantly on the way down.

Gabe felt a warm buzz race through his body. Akon pulsed from the speakers in the corners of the solarium. Dina and six other girls jumped out of the pool and stormed the wet bar, giggling and shrieking as they dragged the boys away to dance. Gabe found himself sandwiched between Dina and the girl who'd offered him a shot earlier. Dover sat on the edge of the pool making out with Melanie while Britney massaged his wet shoulders. His eyes were closed, and he looked totally blissed out.

Gabe closed his eyes, took a deep swallow from the martini glass, and let the throbbing music wash over him. His days of Dumpster-diving were over.

VICTORY IS SWEETEST WHEN YOU'VE KNOWN DEFEAT.

—MALCOLM FORBES

"WHAT THE HELL?"

Gabe's eyes flew open. In the doorway opposite the one they'd entered stood Mack Jacobs—and he was glaring directly at Gabe. Gabe blinked. Mack looked even bigger than he had this afternoon. His muscular, sausagelike arms dangled from the rolled-up sleeves of his blue-and-white striped shirt, which hung unbuttoned and untucked. Athena Brand was peeking over Mack's shoulder. *She* was the third girl to let him juggle her jubblies that night? Didn't she have any pride?

"WHAT ARE YOU LOSERS DOING HERE?" Mack kept his gaze trained on Gabe while pointing at Dover. "This is a party, not a turkey farm. Who let these two nerds in?" He scanned the crowd. Gabe's heart sank as he saw Troy shrug. Was he going to pretend not to know him now?

Mack zeroed in on Dover.

"Where have I seen those corduroys before?" he asked. "Oh, that's right—*on you*. Every day since, like, October. Will you self-destruct if you wear something else? Don't you know that compulsion is one of the first signs of mental illness?"

Gabe snickered. He couldn't help it. He'd always felt the

same way about Dover's cords. Of course, he'd never said anything about it because Dover was his best friend.

Dover turned hurt eyes on him as Britney rose disdainfully from the edge of the pool and walked off. Her perfect, pale, camouflage-clad butt swiveled angrily from side to side. Melanie, meanwhile, slipped into the water and swam over to a cluster of polo players. All over the pool, kids had stopped playing. They stood or treaded water, waiting to see what Mack would do.

Gabe tried to look nonchalant and took a huge gulp of his martini. Immediately he began coughing and spluttering as the clear liquor burned his throat. He knocked the olive from the edge of his glass and sent it bouncing into the pool, where another girl shrieked and swam away from it. Dina threw him a disgusted look. She grabbed the body-shot girl by the hand and stalked off.

Mack turned his gaze back to Gabe. Shaking Athena off, he walked over to where Gabe was standing. Troy and the dark-haired, Speedo-wearing boy stepped aside quickly as he passed. Gabe tried not to quiver as Mack strode up to him, but the sloshing of the remaining liquor in his glass betrayed his nerves.

"Hey, Tweezers." Mack came to a halt before him. "How'd you get out of the Dumpster Mike and Jon threw you in earlier this afternoon?" He flicked Gabe's glasses—hard. "Did you find these in there?"

Dina tittered, and Troy laughed outright. Gabe blushed to the roots of his hair. How had this happened? One minute he and Dover had been ruling the party, and now he couldn't even think of a snappy comeback. He couldn't think about anything at all except getting out of there.

Mack evidently had the same thing on his mind. "Hey," he called, looking over Gabe's shoulder. Gabe turned to see Jon and Mike enter the pool area. He shuddered involuntarily, unable to take his eyes off them as they made their way over to him.

"I'm guessing, since you're here, that you remember me telling you about the party this afternoon," Mack said to Gabe. Gabe nodded miserably. Mack continued. "And do you remember what I asked you?"

"If-if you could count me in." Gabe's voice was a hoarse caricature of its former self. Jon and Mike were flanking him now. He couldn't believe this was happening again.

"Listen," he pleaded, "I'll—We'll be happy to go, won't we, Dover?" He turned to his best friend and read in his face a mixture of hurt, pity, and rage. Dover stayed silent, and Gabe didn't blame him. But he babbled on. "We'll all go, and—"

"'All'?" Mack interrupted. "Did you geeks figure out a way to clone yourselves? Or are your glasses failing you? Because I only see one of him"—he pointed to Dover—"and one of you." Jon laid a heavy hand on one of Gabe's arms. Mike clamped down on the other. Water sloshed over the edges of the pool as the crowd shifted and buzzed. Were they going to throw him in the pool? Or through one of the plateglass windows? Gabe gulped. His throat felt dry and spiky, as though he'd swallowed a cactus.

Unbelievably, Troy came to his rescue. "They brought a girl," he explained. "That's the only reason I even talked to them in the first place."

"A *girl*?" Mack roared with laughter. "A girl *what*? Sheep? Horse? Pig? Cow? Do—" The last word died on his lips as the bathroom door on the other side of the pool opened and Trina stepped out. *A girl robot*, thought Gabe, his heart welling in his chest.

Mack's jaw hung open as Trina shut the door neatly behind her. Her platinum tresses bounced as she walked along the edge of the pool, each click of her silver high-heeled sandals sending up a little splash of water. The blond boy who'd jumped into the pool stared upward, treading water. He wore an expression similar to Mack's, but as Trina passed above him, he stopped treading and began to sink. Spluttering, he brought himself to the surface and gazed thunderstruck after Trina. *Oh, right,* Gabe thought dimly. *No panties.*

Trina touched Dover on the shoulder as she went by, and he stood up without trying to sneak a peek, possibly for the first time in his life. Gabe opened his mouth to speak as she approached, but she passed him without a glance. His heart sank as she swayed up to Mack instead. He couldn't believe it. The Theory of One was so powerful it could even attract a *robot*? And how could she know? Had she seen Athena Brand clinging to him? He looked around for Dina—maybe if he went and stood next to her . . .

"Well, well, well," Mack drawled, addressing Trina's cleavage, "what have we here? Were you hired to babysit these geeks? Because you can babysit *me* any day, darling." He reached out and touched Trina's wrist, and Gabe felt the hairs on the back of his neck rise in anger.

But Trina didn't flinch. In fact, she leaned in closer to Mack and put a hand to his face. Gabe's knees threatened to turn to water.

"Where did you come from?" she purred.

"Um . . . upstairs?" All traces of the former debate hero were vanquished by the force of Trina's considerable beauty.

"What's up there?" She reached inside his shirt and trailed a delicate finger down his bare chest. Gabe felt the martini roiling in his stomach, threatening to make a reappearance.

"The make-out room," Mack replied, his confidence obviously returning. "Why? You wanna go up there now?"

"Yes," Trina said. "I do." And with that she turned and walked over to Gabe. Unbidden, Jon and Mike released his arms and stepped away. Gabe steeled himself. No matter what happened, he wouldn't let her see him crack. And then the whole world vanished, as Trina leaned in . . .

. . . and kissed him. Right on the lips. Her mouth was lush and soft, and Gabe felt every nerve ending in his body erupt in flames as the kiss continued. Forgetting himself, Gabe reached around and placed a gentle hand on the back of Trina's head, his fingers tangling in her long, white-blonde hair. He traced his other hand down her smooth arm until it came to rest on her silk-clad hip. She moved closer and wrapped her arms around him. The kiss became longer, deeper, more passionate, and Gabe's heart beat faster and faster. Finally, Trina broke the kiss and pulled away. Gabe opened his eyes.

All around him, kids whooped and hollered. Troy shook his head admiringly, Jon and Mike had disappeared, and Mack stood openmouthed and red-faced, clenching his fists. Gabe felt like diving into the pool and swimming two hundred laps. *His first kiss!* And it had been amazing. Not just because it had happened in front of the whole school—the whole city, practically—but because it had been with Trina. His dream girl.

She reached out to take his hand. Ignoring Mack completely, she led Gabe toward the very steps down which Mack had come.

The steps to the make-out room.

As he climbed the stairs, he heard Troy shout, "Give it up for Gabe, everyone!" The sound of thunderous applause followed.

Practically floating on air, Gabe followed Trina down the hall, too stoked to be nervous about what was going to happen next. Who cared? He was infatuated! No, he was in love! He was in—

"—trouble." Trina reached for the doorknob to the make-out room, identifiable by a red construction-paper heart taped to the door.

"What?"

"I said, we're in trouble." Trina yanked hard on the knob. "I saw the people from the SUV through the window," she explained. "I kissed you so they couldn't see our faces. We have to hide. Quick, help me open this door."

I CAN'T TALK, I CAN'T THINK. MY FEELINGS BURN
INSIDE OF ME.

—BLACK FLAG

OH. GABE CAME BACK DOWN TO EARTH WITH A THUD. AS WHAT Trina had just said sank in, he realized he didn't have time to be depressed. The people chasing them had guns—they had to *hide*!

He joined Trina in rattling the doorknob. The door was locked—but hadn't Mack said he'd just come from there? Did he keep it locked so his various conquests wouldn't catch him red-handed with the competition?

Just as Gabe was about to give up and suggest they seek shelter somewhere else, the door flew open. "Hey, man!" a pale, tousled, black-haired boy wearing a T-shirt with a skull on it greeted him. He was busy refastening a brass bullet belt around his hips. A girl with spiky hair dyed to look like leopard spots came up behind him and wrapped her arms around his chest.

"Have fun!" she said in a cigarette-husky voice, winking at Trina. The boy smiled happily at Gabe and stumbled forward out the door. Gabe could hear him and his girlfriend chattering happily as they descended the stairs.

He turned back to Trina, who was still standing in the hall.

Seconds ago, he had felt like there wasn't enough time. Now, every second felt like eternity.

"Well," he said awkwardly, "I guess we should go in."

Trina nodded. Gabe remembered his manners and gestured politely for her to enter the room. She did, and he followed, shutting the door behind them.

"Well, at least we know it locks!" He tried to lighten the mood. He jiggled the knob. Then he stuck his hands in his pockets and surveyed the room . . .

. . . or tried to. There wasn't very much light. A small lamp glowed on a dresser across the room, and moonlight filtered in through the filmy white curtains blowing at the window, which was partially open, but that was it. A wardrobe hulked in the corner, and some clothes were draped over a chair. Gabe picked up one of the garments and fingered it. It was a pair of man's slacks, way too geriatric for Mack and his brother—and also way too small.

Gabe moved over to the dresser. There were a few pictures on it, some old-looking photos of a mom and dad and two cute, innocent-looking blond kids who looked to be about five and eight. A dish held some jewelry. It dawned on Gabe that this was Mack's parents' room. Gabe vaguely remembered Mr. Jacobs as a mild, diminutive man who had amassed a fortune developing gaming software. How he'd managed to sire a couple of brutes like Mack and his brother, Gabe would never know.

He turned around and finally did what he'd been avoiding doing since they entered the room. He looked at the bed. It was huge—king-size, Gabe guessed—with mounds of plush pillows piled against a carved wooden headboard. Despite the fact that tons of kids had probably already been in here tonight, the covers were only slightly rumpled.

Gabe's heart began to pound uncontrollably. He turned away from the bed and, to distract himself, yanked open the dresser drawer directly underneath the little light. A bright strip of turquoise lay across a neat stack of men's boxer shorts. *Condoms.* Gabe immediately shut the drawer, grateful for the low light.

Trina hadn't moved since they entered. Now he locked eyes with her from across the bed. He was willing to bet on it: Never had he felt more uncomfortable in his life.

"So." He silently cursed himself as his voice cracked painfully in the middle of the *o*. "Uh, what do you think we should do now?"

Trina hesitated a moment before answering. "I think we should change clothes so that the people chasing us have a harder time recognizing us." She gestured at her own abbreviated outfit. "I think this is pretty conspicuous."

Gabe nodded his agreement. Secretly, he was fascinated: How did Trina know her tiny dress and high heels made her stand out? Had she been programmed to understand complex social mores? He turned the question over in his mind. If she had been programmed to back out of a driveway without looking behind her, there was no telling what else she was capable of. He wished his dad were here so he could ask about the creation of this fascinating creature.

Across the room, Trina made an approving sound as she held up a creamy angora sweater. Gabe shook his head to clear it. He was alone in a room with a sexy girl wearing no panties and a giant bed. Why was he thinking about his dad?

"Are you finding anything?" she asked him, sashaying over to the full-length mirror that hung on the inside of the bedroom door to hold the sweater up to her chest.

"Um, not yet." Gabe rummaged blindly through the dresser. He really hoped the pants that had been flung over the chair weren't indicative of Mr. Jacobs's taste. If he was going to be shot dead in front of a beautiful girl, whether or not she was a robot, he didn't want to die in the socks and Sansabelts of a forty-five-year-old man.

So far, he wasn't having any luck. Drawer after drawer was turning up starched, creased shirts, folded and banded, and hideous multicolored sweaters that looked as though they had been knit from the wool of sheep fed an exclusive diet of blotter acid. Gabe had only recently learned about the existence of this drug in health class. Between that and crabs, he was very glad he hadn't been alive in the sixties, the ancient decade in which he assumed Mr. Jacobs had been born.

Finally, the last drawer yielded some decent clothes. Well,

decent compared to everything Gabe had found so far. He held up an old Princeton University T-shirt and a pair of faded Levi's. Judging from the splotches that adorned them, these were Mr. Jacobs's painting clothes, but that was just fine with him.

"All right," he said. "I'm good to go."

"Me too." Trina triumphantly held up a pair of lacy pink panties.

Gabe dropped the T-shirt. "Is that all you're going to wear?" he gasped, fumbling to retrieve it.

"No, silly!" Trina giggled. She pointed to the bed, where the sweater and a short summer dress with flowers on it lay.

"Oh." Gabe felt a curious mixture of disappointment and relief. Then he felt the familiar feeling of awkwardness steal over him again.

"So . . ." he began, looking about. There was nowhere to change—there weren't even any closets! They must be out in the hall. Now what?

Trina answered his unspoken question. "Okay. Turn around, and don't peek."

Gabe's heart filled with warmth. She trusted him! She trusted him not to look!

"Okay," he said gallantly, and then added, "you don't look either!"

She giggled, and they turned their backs on each other. Gabe tried not to think too hard about the rustle of fabric against skin he heard behind him, and instead focused on wrestling with a knotted shoelace. He had just stripped off his T-shirt and jeans and was down to his underwear when he heard footsteps in the hall. He froze.

". . . must be up here somewhere," a female voice said.

Gabe's blood turned to ice in his veins. He heard the footsteps stop and a door creak open.

"This one's an office or something," the girl said.

Gabe's hands trembled as he reached for Mr. Jacobs's jeans. Maybe it was just another couple looking for the make-out room. Maybe they were looking for the bathroom. Maybe—

"Turn the lights on," a gruff male voice instructed. "And remember, we want them alive."

Gabe dropped the jeans. Completely forgetting that he wasn't supposed to turn around, he whirled to face Trina. Gulping, he took in the sight before him.

Trina had also frozen at the sound of the man's voice. She was standing with one hand on the back of the chair, wearing nothing but the pink lacy panties and matching bra she must have found. Barefoot, she was closer to his height, and this somehow made Gabe feel even more protective of her. He felt something else, too, but he wasn't going to let himself think about it just now.

They remained motionless, staring at each other. Out in the hall, the man spoke again.

"Nothing. Check the closets."

More sounds of doors being opened and closed; more footsteps, and then they were at the door. Gabe sucked in his breath as he saw the faceted glass knob turn. *No!*

"Damn," the girl said. "It's locked."

"I'll handle it," the man said. There was a scraping sound as he began to pick the lock.

Oh my God! thought Gabe. *He's going to pick the lock! We're going to be caught!*

He opened his mouth with every intention of communicating this thought to Trina, but he never got the chance to, because the next thing he knew, he was flat on his back on the bed, with Trina hovering above him, the light from the dresser casting a warm halo about her white-blonde hair.

"Shhhhhh," she cautioned. Gabe nodded weakly. Then he heard the sound of the door giving way, and suddenly Trina was kissing him—kissing him in a way that made the kiss they'd shared at the pool seem like a peck on the lips. Gabe felt her tongue at his teeth. Was she going to French him?

Unsure of what to do, Gabe opened his mouth slightly. He didn't want her to be greeted by a gaping cavern in case he'd been wrong. This way, he could just pretend it had been an accident if she didn't want to do it.

She did. Gently, she slid her tongue between his lips. Gabe thought he might explode. Leaning forward, she almost covered his body with hers.

Light flooded the room, and Gabe heard a man's voice

gasp, "Oh . . . I'm so sorry." But he didn't care. Trina's long hair curtained his face completely, and she moaned faintly as she writhed sexily atop him. At first Gabe didn't know where to put his hands, but he settled for the smooth curve of her waist. They kissed and kissed and kissed some more. The rolling contact of Trina's hips was driving Gabe wild. He seriously thought he might lose control if they didn't stop soon.

And then the door closed, and the light went away, and the footsteps went away, and Trina sat up.

"Phew," she said, smiling at him and flipping her hair back. "That was close!"

YOU'VE GOT ME, GIRL, ON THE RUNAROUND.

—ROXY MUSIC

GABE LAY ON HIS BACK AMID THE TANGLED SHEETS IN A DAZE, HIS thoughts running wild. He was in love! And Trina was in love with him! Happily, he imagined himself walking to school with Trina, carrying her books, laughing with her as they ate lunch in the cafeteria, making out on the school steps with everybody watching . . .

No, he reminded himself. *She's a robot. Robots don't go to school. Or eat.* He drifted back into the fantasy. This time Trina was wearing her hot maid outfit and helping him rewire a microprocessor, pausing every few minutes to kiss him.

He looked up at Trina, who was still straddling him, and upon seeing her face, his happy glow evaporated and was replaced by a feeling of worry. Trina looked uncomfortable— almost sad.

"Hey." Gabe struggled to sit up. "What's wrong? The bad guys left! Everything's okay!"

"It's not that." Trina moved jerkily off him. He sat up fully. Trina dropped down next to him, her head drooping.

"I'm losing power," she explained. "I need to recharge."

Gabe went cold. He had studied robotics for years—how

had he failed to foresee this? Hell, any idiot who owned an iPod could have seen this coming! He watched in horror as Trina slowly stretched out on the bed, burying her face in the pillows. As she shifted position, the top of her tattoo peeked briefly over the back of her panties. Looking at it, Gabe realized he had no idea what kind of power system she operated on. He needed to ask her before she shut down completely!

"Hey." He shook her gently. She looked up at him through huge, brown eyes, and Gabe marveled again at how human she seemed. Shaking the thought off, he took her chin in his hand and gently stroked her cheek. "What kind . . . what kind of batteries do you take?" he asked. God, this was surreal! "Can I raid the house looking for flashlights to strip? Or is it the same kind a Mac takes? What kind of port do you have and"—he swallowed nervously—"where is it?"

She smiled weakly at his obvious discomfort, and his heart melted a little bit more.

"So la—" she closed her eyes.

Panic-stricken, Gabe grasped her by the shoulder. "What? What did you say?" He shook her lightly, then a little harder, but got no response. Had she said *so long*? As in, *good-bye*?

"Hey!"

Gabe whirled around as light flooded the room. Dover stood in the doorway; his corduroys still looked wet, but he had regained his T-shirt.

"What the hell?" Dover looked from the underwear-clad

Gabe to Trina in her bra and panties, to the unmade bed and back again. "Wow, some friend you are. Acting all high and mighty when *I* wanted to do stuff with her, when it turns out you just wanted her for yourself. Well, now it's my turn!"

"No!" Gabe said. "It's not what you think!"

"It's not what I think?" Dover banged his fist against the wardrobe, jealousy and rage plain on his handsome features. "You guys are practically naked in bed in the make-out room and *it's not what I think?"*

"I *wish* it was what you think!" Gabe said in frustration. "She only kissed me in the first place because she saw those people who were chasing us through the window," he explained ruefully. "That's why she dragged me up here. We were changing into other clothes so we wouldn't be recognized, when they showed up. She just pretended to be making out with me so they couldn't see our faces," he finished.

Dover went pale under the hallway lights. Stepping completely inside the room, he closed the door behind him with a click. *"What?* Those people in the SUV are here?"

"You didn't see them? I was wondering where you were." This wasn't entirely true: Gabe had forgotten everything, including his own name, the moment Trina kissed him, but it was what he would have wanted Dover to say to him in a similar situation.

Dover smirked. "Yeah, I *bet* you were."

Gabe hung his head.

"Whatever," Dover said. "I *definitely* wouldn't have thought about you! Anyway," he continued, turning serious, "I didn't see them, but right after you left, Melanie pulled me back in the water, so maybe that's where I was when they came in." He stared at Trina's prone form. "Do you think they're still here?"

"I don't know," Gabe admitted. "But we've got to get out of here. Even if they're gone, I don't really feel like running into Mack again."

Dover was still staring at Trina. "Wow," he said, "you must really be an animal in the sack! Is she . . . passed out?"

Gabe blushed. "No," he said, "it's worse than that."

Dover's mouth fell open. "You mean she's *dead*?"

"No, I don't mean she's dead. She's a robot, for crying out loud! She's run out of power, and we have to find some way to recharge her."

Dover whistled. "What kind of batteries does she take?"

"That's what I tried to ask her right before she shut down. I managed to eliminate a couple options, but I couldn't under-stand what she told me."

"What did she say?" Dover asked.

"It sounded like 'so long'—like she was saying good-bye almost," Gabe said sadly.

"'So long'?"

"Yeah, just 'so-la' and she was out."

"So-la . . . Oh my God!" Dover shouted. "Remember the weird lights in the centrifuge we found her in?"

"Yeah, sure," Gabe said. "Query: What's your point?"

"Don't you see?" Dover cried. "They were just like the kind you find in a tanning bed! *Solar!* Not 'so long'!"

"Yes! Rechargeable! We're in!" The two friends high-fived. Then Gabe looked down at his tighty whities.

"Um . . . can you hand me those jeans lying on the floor? I'm feeling kind of . . . naked right now."

Dover snickered and handed him the pants. "Hey, at least you've got hair on your chest now." He leaned in and peered exaggeratedly at Gabe's scrawny, pale chest. "Oh, wait, no you don't. Those were shadows."

"Hey!" Gabe smacked him. Then he had an idea. "Do you want to help me dress Trina?"

"Hell yes! I mean, I'd much rather *un*dress her, but I'll take any chance I can get to touch that hot bod!"

Instantly, Gabe regretted his decision. "Okay," he said, "but no groping."

Dover drew himself up. "What kind of monster do you think I am?"

"Well, considering you were ready to have sex with her before we even booted her up . . ."

"Okay, okay," Dover said. "I'll be a perfect gentleman. Hand me her dress."

Reluctantly, Gabe handed over the dress Trina had chosen from Mrs. Jacobs's wardrobe, and together they managed to get her into it.

"Wow." Gabe fumbled with the hook-and-eye closure at the back of the dress, "girls' clothes are tough to get on."

"They're even tougher to get off," Dover pointed out. Then he looked thoughtful. "Maybe this would be a good time to learn how to take a girl's bra off with one hand. We could—"

"No," Gabe cut him off, "we couldn't. Hand me her sweater, will you?" He slipped her arms into the garment while Dover fumbled with her sandals: Mrs. Jacobs's shoes were all too small.

"All right." Gabe eased Trina back onto the bed. "Our turn. I took the only pair of jeans, so it looks like your choices are business suit or banana hammock. Or perhaps a subtle combination of the two?"

Dover rolled his eyes. "I don't know if you've noticed this." He pointed to the jeans and Princeton T-shirt, "but those are almost identical to the clothes you're ditching."

Gabe looked at the corner where his old T-shirt and jeans lay. "You're right," he agreed, reaching for his own jeans. "It's not like anyone's looking at us anyway."

"Weeeell, I *did* get Melanie's number."

"Ha, golden!" Gabe smiled broadly. Then he turned serious. "How are we going to get out of here without anyone seeing us?"

"One of the cheerleaders puked in the pool, so that area should be deserted. It smells pretty bad."

"Ugh, but what about people outside? They can still see in," Gabe pointed out. "And that walkway is glass, too."

"Good point. I guess we're gonna have to go down to the other end of the hall."

Carefully, he slid his arms underneath Trina and lifted her from the bed. He staggered a little under the deadweight and then felt a glow rush through him. Trina felt warm and soft in his arms.

"This looks really bad, man. It looks like she's totally passed out." Trina's arms hung down limply.

Gabe shifted her slightly so that her head, which had been thrown back, was shifted forward, her hair hiding her eyes.

"It's going to be even worse when she's fully powered down," he said. "Right now she's in ECM, but she'll be able to interface a little bit, perform emergency responses."

"ECM?" Dover looked confused.

"Energy conservation mode," Gabe explained. "Executive decision: We're going out through the pool room and the backyard. If anybody asks us, we're just gonna say she had too much to drink and we're taking her home."

Dover nodded and turned toward the door. Opening it, he scanned the hallway. "Clear," he reported, stepping into the hall. Gabe followed him, and with Dover staying a slight distance ahead so he could act as lookout, they descended the stairs into the pool room, which, mercifully, had been darkened following the vomiting incident, perhaps as a warning that the room was no longer an available partying space. It was an unnecessary precaution.

"Phew," Gabe said as they made their way along the pool's edge. "It smells like she was drinking Frankenberry-flavored Mad Dog."

"They make that?" Dover paused at the breezeway.

"NO, they don't frigging make that," Gabe hissed. "Get a move on. My arms are getting tired."

The two boys made their way through the breezeway and out to the kitchen, which led to the backyard. The party was raging full throttle now, with a lot of kids completely blitzed or passed out, so, as Dover had speculated, they didn't attract too much attention . . .

. . . until they opened the door to the backyard. It had been jammed when Gabe checked it out before. Now the displaced partiers from the pool mingled wetly with jocks, goth girls, cheer-leaders, and a handful of hairy-chested, slightly older boys who were dressed in the styles of 1975. *A band?* Gabe thought vaguely. Candles in glass containers burned on every available surface, giving the patio the aura of a dying sun. If he'd been in better shape, Gabe would have thought that was kinda cool. As it was, he longed for pitch-blackness and the cover it would provide.

"All riiiiiight, dude! Score! Way to *go!*" a drunken skater hollered from atop the lip of the half-pipe Mack had bragged about that afternoon. The boy pointed at Trina. All over the backyard, heads began to swivel.

Gabe tried frantically to pick up the pace as the boy's friends joined him in whooping and hollering. At least they didn't have to pass the keg, he thought, glancing toward the far corner of the patio.

He froze. The blonde girl from the SUV was staring right at him. She was surrounded by eager high-school boys, all vying for her attention—the gray-haired man appeared to be nowhere in sight. The girl said something to the boy nearest her, handed him her cup, and began making her way through the throng.

Gabe felt a tug at his arm. Dover.

"What are you *doing*?" he hissed. Then his gaze followed Gabe's. "Oh my God. *Run!*"

Abandoning all pretense of calm, the boys broke for the edge of the lawn, Dover sprinting and Gabe stumbling behind him.

"Yeah, you'd better hurry!" the drunken skater called from the top of the ramp. "Before someone comes along and steals her!"

Jerk, Gabe thought as he fumbled with the locks on the Beavle, *you don't know how right you are.*

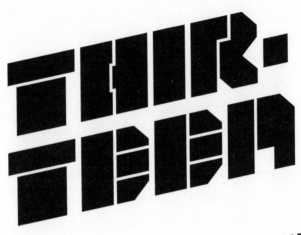

THIR-
TEEN

WHAT MAKES THEM SPARKLE? WHAT MAKES
THEM SHINE? WHAT MAKES THOSE EYES OF
YOURS LOOK INTO MINE?

—HÜSKER DÜ

AS QUICKLY AND CAREFULLY AS HE COULD, GABE LAID TRINA down in the backseat.

"I dunno," Dover commented behind him, "I kinda miss the no-panties look."

"Will you shut up and get in the car?" Gabe adjusted Trina's skirt and slammed the door. Bolting to the driver's side, he jumped into the front seat, slid the key into the ignition, and pulled away from the curb, slamming the door as he did so.

"That woman is on the front lawn, but I don't see the guy," Dover said as Gabe executed a fast U-turn and sped away from the house. "Damn, that was close," Dover continued as he turned back around in his seat. "Good thing we didn't make a left when we went out the back door. We'd never have made it."

The streets flew by as Gabe frantically tried to put some distance between them and their followers.

"Where are we going?" Dover finally asked.

"To a tanning salon."

"*Now?*" Dover exclaimed. "It's after midnight!"

"That place in the strip mall on Pleasant with the glass front, where the waiting room looks like a sauna? Golden Girls Tanning? I think it's twenty-four hours."

"The one where they're always cranking oldies through the outside speakers to lure in middle-aged ladies?"

"That's the one," Gabe sped up to catch a yellow light.

"Wow, I bet there are some B-A-B-E-S there at this hour," Dover speculated. "You know, strippers just getting off work, drunk college girls. Hey, drunk college girls!" He indicated Trina. "We'll blend right in!"

"I said, be quiet!" Gabe leaned forward to peer at a blinking light on the dash. *It couldn't be . . .*

"Damn, you're tense!" Dover flung his hands up in exasperation. "*You* were the one who had the bright idea of letting people think we were carrying her out of there wasted. Now you're—"

"*Now we're out of gas!*" Gabe shouted as the car began to slow.

"WHAT?" Dover leaned across the steering wheel. "No way! Let me see!"

"Move your head!" Gabe shoved his friend. "I have to get us over to the curb or we're just gonna stall out in the middle of the road." Fortunately, there weren't any other cars in sight at this late hour.

Gabe's muscles strained as he fought to turn the steering wheel. "Shit!" he gasped. "The power steering's gone! Help me out!"

Dover reached over and yanked hard on the wheel. "Nnggh!" Slowly, the car drifted to the curb. Gabe slung the transmission into park and stared at the gas gauge. Then he gazed out at the dark boulevard. A graveyard sat dim and silent on the right; a few houses were to their left. Far ahead, the lights of a little strip mall glowed. He could just make out the blurred fluorescent shape of a corner gas station. So things could be worse. *But still . . .*

"I can't believe we didn't notice this!" He slammed his hands against the steering wheel, sending lightning bolts of pain through his forearms. He didn't care. He felt like punishing himself. How could he have been so stupid?

"Look." Dover's tone was soothing. "I agree this sucks, but it wasn't like we didn't have more important things to worry about. Plus . . ." He nodded toward the backseat, where Trina lay slumped. "You weren't driving."

Gabe turned to look at Trina. Her white-blonde hair spilled over her face, all but obscuring it from view. It was funny, Gabe thought, how he could still tell she was beautiful, even though he could barely see her face.

"All right," he said, without taking his eyes off her. "You're gonna have to go get gas."

"*I'm* gonna go get gas? Man, you are greedy with that girl! How about *you* go get the gas and I stay here with her!" Dover swiveled in his seat to face Gabe, fists clenched.

"No way," Gabe said. "You still have your phone, remember?"

Dover crossed his arms and shook his head slowly. "You're gonna have to do better than that. It's out of juice."

"What? Since when?" His dad's robot was on ECM in the backseat, the car was out of gas, and Dover's phone was dead. Technology, which he usually considered his second-best friend, was really sucking. And when people with guns were after them, it wasn't really the best time to be let down.

"I think it died sometime after we left the gas station." Dover yanked the iPhone from his pocket and stared at its dead black screen. "Or maybe even before. Anyway," he continued, "I was gonna see if I could jack a charge at the party, but . . ." He shrugged.

"Well," Gabe dragged a tired hand across his eyes, "I guess that explains why my dad hasn't tried to call us on it." He looked at Dover. "You're still going to get gas, though."

"What the hell!" Dover's expression darkened. "You just don't trust me! It's okay for you to be . . . to be naked and grinding on her in the bedroom—"

"I wasn't naked, and I *wasn't*, as you so romantically put it, 'grinding on her'!"

"I'm your best friend." Dover pounded his fist on the glove compartment for emphasis. "Why don't you trust me?"

"*Because* you're my best friend," Gabe said. "Dude, I *know* you!"

"You *think* you know me." Dover pushed the car door open, jumped out, and slammed it shut. He stuck his head in the open window. His expression was hurt and angry. "But maybe you don't." He stomped around to the trunk and yanked it open. Rummaging about, he withdrew a bright red plastic container.

"Dover . . ." Gabe began. Dover slammed the trunk shut without looking at him. His shadow brushed past the side of the car. Gabe twisted back to face the windshield and watched him walk away in the white blaze of the headlights. Sighing, he reached down and shut them off, switching the hazards on instead. The ticking sound they made as they flashed on and off was somehow soothing. He watched the yellow and red hues flicker across the rearview mirror for a while.

"Ooooohhh . . ."

Gabe jumped. *What the—?*

He turned around. Trina was struggling to sit up.

"Heyheyhey!" he said. "You don't wanna drain what little power you have left."

Trina moaned sadly and dropped back to the seat. Gabe looked at her for a moment. His heart felt weirdly constricted. He let his gaze travel over her curvy form. She lay huddled on her side and, in the short, flowered dress, seemed especially vulnerable. He watched her sweater-clad shoulder rise and fall. *What a miracle of engineering,* he thought. And then that thought was overridden by another. *She looks scared.*

Moving slowly, he opened the door and got out. He walked around the front of the car. The vehicle's eye-catching, pale-green color was muted in the darkness. He looked down the boulevard. He couldn't see Dover anymore. Leaning down, he opened the rear passenger-side door of the Beavle and slid in, shutting the door to keep the chilly night air at bay.

"Hey . . ." He laid a hand on her arm. The sweater was soft, and he could feel the warmth of her body radiating through it. He closed his eyes. How was that possible? Was her internal temperature controlled to feel like 98.6 degrees? He opened them. He was alone with a beautiful girl in a broken-down car. Why was he thinking about dumb shit like that?

Trina shifted, her hair falling away from her face. Her eyes locked with his and she smiled weakly. "H-hey." The velvety fabric slid from underneath Gabe's hand as she struggled to sit up.

"Are you sure that's a good idea?" He tried not to let her see how anxious he was, but he really didn't want her to use up any more energy than was necessary. Who knew how long they'd be out here? What if the people who were chasing them caught up with them?

"It's okay," she said, pulling her knees up on the seat and tugging her dress down to cover as much of her silky thighs as she could. Gabe tried not to stare. "I just have to conserve as much energy as I can right now," she continued, "because I only have enough for one big event, or for another hour at this level."

"One . . . big event?" Was she referring to her 'mission'? Whatever that was? "Like . . . ?"

Trina laughed. "Like . . . playing water polo for a few minutes. Or . . . running. Anything that would make a person's heart rate speed up."

Running. Gabe shuddered. He hoped they wouldn't have to—that the black SUV would stay far, far away. Then he thought of something.

"When you went to the bathroom at the party . . . uuuh-hhhh . . ." He trailed off. He had been about to ask her why a robot would need to use the bathroom. But what kind of guy asked a girl who looked like this—hell, any girl!—what she was doing in the bathroom? His face burned in the darkness.

Trina placed a reassuring hand on his leg. Gabe tried not to hyperventilate.

"You want to know what I was doing in the bathroom." Her brown eyes searched his blue ones. "Because I'm a robot, and robots don't need to go to the bathroom."

"Uh . . . well . . . yeah." How weird was it that she knew she was a robot? He didn't think he would ever get used to it.

"I knew my batteries were draining," she explained. "And I didn't know how long we would be at the party. I didn't want to waste energy walking around and talking to people, and I needed to find a place to take a break."

"You played party possum!"

Her pretty brow furrowed. "Party possum?"

131

"That's what Dover and I call it when you're at a party but you can't deal with it," explained Gabe. "You just disappear for a while. Like you did."

"Oh." Trina laughed. "Do you go to a lot of parties?"

Gabe wanted to squirm in embarrassment, but her hand was on his leg. "No," he admitted. "I mean, birthday parties when you're a kid, and family stuff. But that party we were just at . . . that was our first real one."

Trina smiled. "Mine too!"

Gabe felt warm inside. He hadn't thought of that. Of course it had been her first party. So technically . . . they had gone to their first party together. The thought that they were in some way on equal footing made him feel bold.

"So," he said. "Is it weird . . . being a robot who . . . a robot that looks like a person?"

Instantly, Gabe regretted the question. Trina looked sad, and she hung her head a little bit, like she had back in the bedroom when she'd been losing power. But then she straightened up.

"It's . . . hard to explain," she said slowly. "I guess you could say I feel more like a person who knows she's a robot. Like, for example . . ." She met his gaze squarely. "I like being around people. And I like some people better than others. But I don't know why."

"I guess nobody knows why." Gabe's heart beat faster. Did she like him better than other people? "So that's pretty human." He grinned at her. "And you have a name, too, not, like, a number or something."

"It's an acronym," she said. Gabe remembered the letters stamped across the hard drive. How did she know?

"Do you know what it means?" he asked, trying to sound nonchalant.

She shook her head. "I think it means 'This Robot Is Nearly Alive.'" She gave a wistful little laugh. "At least, that's how I feel."

They were quiet for a moment. Dover's window up front was still rolled down. The road outside was silent. It was too early in the spring for crickets or peepers, and too late at night for lots of traffic. Trina shifted closer to Gabe. He held his breath as she lowered her head onto his shoulder. For a minute, Gabe didn't say anything. Then . . .

"I like you," he finally said.

Trina didn't reply. Gabe began to panic. Had he said too much? Been too forward? Had he misread her feelings for him? Was he stupid to even think robots *had* feelings?

Trina's hand, which had been resting on his thigh, slid off and bounced against the seat.

Powered down.

Partly, he felt nervous. What if the man and woman who were chasing them showed up now? Would he be able to lift her?

But he also felt happy. Trina had said that she only had

enough energy left for a couple minutes—if she engaged in an activity that made a person's heart pound faster. She hadn't done any running or jumping. In fact, she had barely moved. Did that mean her heart—or whatever his dad had created to take its place—had been pounding just as hard as his?

He was just contemplating this fact when a hand landed heavily on the window next to him.

"Aaahhhh!" Gabe shrieked. The door opened, and Dover looked inside.

"Hey, man," he said cheerily, "sorry I was so—hey!" His expression changed as he took in the sight of Trina slumped against Gabe. Dover shook his head. "You really are a dick, you know that?" he said. He slammed the door and went around to the back. Gabe could hear him tinkering with the gas cap and then the liquid flooding in.

He eased himself away from Trina and laid her back down across the seat. Shutting the door, he went back around the front of the car. Dover slid into the passenger seat just as Gabe put the key in the ignition.

"Hey," Gabe said. "Thanks for going to get the gas."

Dover just grunted. Sighing, Gabe turned the key. The Beavle sprang to life. They were off.

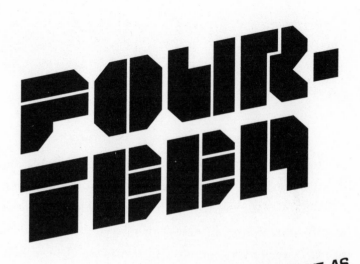

FOUR-
TEEN

A CLOUDY DAY OR A LITTLE SUNSHINE HAVE AS
GREAT AN INFLUENCE ON MANY CONSTITUTIONS
AS THE MOST RECENT BLESSINGS OR MISFOR-
TUNES.

—JOSEPH ADDISON

DOVER TWIDDLED WITH THE KNOBS ON THE STEREO AS THE CAR sped toward the tanning salon. Gabe twiddled the knobs on his own emotions. He didn't feel like he'd done anything wrong by hanging out with Trina. Why should he have to explain himself? But then he remembered that he hadn't trusted Dover to stay behind with her. He thought of how Dover must have felt when he found them in the backseat, and he relented.

"Trina powered up after you left." He pulled up to a stop sign, not quite stopping before he rolled through it. Milton called this California stopping. He was, unsurprisingly, adamantly against it.

"Oh, you rebooted her so you wouldn't feel guilty about feeling her up when she was passed out?" Dover stared straight ahead.

"No!" Gabe shouted. "She said she had some kind of reserves left! And I *didn't* feel her up. Not that I wouldn't have liked to," he added in the spirit of honesty. "But she just wanted to talk."

Dover snorted. "Girls. What did she want to talk about?"

"Well, mostly about what it's like to be a robot but also a person."

"You mean, 'but also a smokin' hot babe'? With boobs she can play with anytime she wants?" Dover asked. "Well?"

"I didn't find out very much." Gabe ignored the boobs comment. "Since she avoided the question earlier when I asked her about her mission, I tried to be more, uh, diplomatic this time . . . but it didn't really work."

"Well, she's sure not a maid," Dover said. "Unless those people with guns are her employers and they're mad she doesn't do windows."

The corners of Gabe's mouth twitched. "I don't think it should take us more than half an hour to recharge her," he said, turning into the Golden Girls parking lot. "I guess we can ask her more questions then." He parked the car. Climbing out, he went around and reached into the backseat. He lifted Trina out while Dover ran ahead to get the door.

As it turned out, Dover was wrong about the tanning salon being filled with wine-cooler-fueled college girls. The only other person present in the salon was an alarmingly well-built man in his late forties sporting carefully manicured stubble and, as the boys learned when he stepped out from behind the slatted-wood counter, a very short pair of bright red running shorts.

"Welcome! I'm Rick," he shouted over the pulsing tones of

some ancient new wave song, extending his hand to Dover. "I'll be your experience guide."

"'Experience guide'?" Dover repeated, mopping sweat from his brow. He looked over at Gabe.

Gabe, holding Trina in his arms, was busy taking in their surroundings. The waiting room *did* look like a sauna: The walls, floor, and counter were all made from dark, unvarnished wood. Blue neon tubes ran the length of the ceiling, and a neon palm tree glowed in one corner. Several real, tropical-looking plants crowded around what looked like a charcoal grill near the counter. A video screen hanging from the ceiling showed a bunch of overly bronzed guys wearing linen pants, frolicking on a yacht and throwing buckets of hot-pink paint at a nearly naked girl.

"Yes." Rick grabbed a can of Mountain Dew from behind the counter and took a healthy swig. "Your Golden Girls guru, if you will. We specialize in the total package. Tanning, toning, turning on—it's all possible here," he said, gesturing broadly around the room.

Gabe shifted uncomfortably. Trina was starting to feel heavy, and it was really hot in here. He wished he could get a hand free to get the sweat out of his eyes, but he couldn't risk setting Trina down and letting Rick see just how incapacitated she was.

Rick didn't seem to notice. He chugged deeply from the Mountain Dew can, then took the lid off the grill, revealing a pile of rocks, onto which he emptied the rest of the contents of the can. The rocks hissed as the liquid hit them, and a sickly, sweet-smelling steam arose from them. No wonder it was so hot in here!

"So," Rick continued, tossing the can into a plastic waste-basket decorated with pink flamingos, "how can I be of service?"

"Well, uh . . ." Gabe began.

Dover came to his rescue.

"His sister is supposed to be in a wedding tomorrow." He indicated Gabe and Trina. "She's obviously pretty tan, but she just wanted to get a little boost before the ceremony, y'know?" he continued, speaking quickly. "But the thing is, she's been partying a little hard and—"

"Say no more." Rick held up his hand. "She reminds me of myself at that age." Turning on one Adidas-clad heel, he led them down a wood-paneled hallway with a row of doors on the left-hand side. He pushed one of the doors open: Inside the tiny room, a tanning bed stood against one wall. A terry-cloth robe hung on a hook, and a small shelf held a pair of glasses that looked as though they were made out of two plastic spoons fused together.

"Now," Rick cautioned, "I've set the machine to cycle off after twenty minutes. You can wait out front if you like, or there are benches in the spray-tan room a couple doors down."

"We'll wait in the spray-tan room," Gabe said. "Thanks, Rick."

"No prob. I'll be out front if you need me." Rick moon-walked out of the room.

"Okay." Gabe breathed a sigh of relief as he eased Trina onto the tanning bed in a sitting position. "Help me get her sweater off."

"Finally I'm around for the good part! You know," Dover said, "I think it would be a good idea if we took *everything* off. You don't know how that will affect her charging."

"In fact, I do know," Gabe snapped. "We found her wearing a maid's outfit, remember? And she seemed to work just fine after that." In fact, Gabe was dying to see her naked, but he didn't want Dover to see her, too.

Together, they quickly removed her sweater, folding it and placing it on the shelf where the glasses had been; these they placed carefully over her eyes before shutting the lid to the tanning bed. As they left, closing the door behind them, they heard the bed switch on with a hum, and a bluish glow seeped from underneath the door.

"Come on," Dover said. "I've always wondered how that spray-tan stuff works."

The spray-tan room was a bright, electric blue; the walls appeared to be formed from molded plastic. The floor was tiled, with a drain in the middle. Gabe felt as though he was standing inside the world's biggest shower. A bench sat along one wall of the room; a black plastic strip lined two other walls at about chest height, and nozzles were situated inside each strip every three feet or so. The room smelled of chemicals.

Gabe sat down on the bench. He looked around for the

controls. The last thing he wanted was an accidental spray tan.

Dover sat down beside him. "I can't believe people pay for this shit."

"I know. I mean, how long does it last?"

"Let's find out!" Dover jumped up. "How dark do you want it?"

"What? No!" Gabe said. "We're not getting *spray tans* while we wait for Trina to boot up."

"Why not?" Dover asked. "It's not like we have anything else to do. Unless you want to get a *real* tan. But I remember how red you were after just one day at camp last summer."

Gabe did too. His nickname had been "the Blister," and not even Dover had been able to refrain from using it.

"I don't want *any* kind of tan," he retorted. "We need to be on our guard in case those people who were chasing us show up. It already sucks that we can't wait in the same room she's in."

"Okay, fine," Dover said. "Let's go back into the tanning booth and practice taking Trina's bra off."

"Will you stop talking about taking her clothes off all the time? Can't you think of anything else?"

"No!" Dover shouted. "I can't! And stop being so possessive— it's not like she's your girlfriend or something!"

"Whatever! I'm responsible for getting her home in one piece!"

"If you really cared about getting her home," Dover countered, "we wouldn't be here! She was *out*, man! We could have just driven her back to your house and put her back in her little pod, or whatever, and your dad would never have been the wiser! You don't really want to take her home—you want her powered back up so you can make out with her some more! You're giving me all this grief for wanting to have sex with her, when you want the same thing yourself!"

"I do *not*!" Gabe was red with rage. "In case you haven't noticed, we're being followed by people with guns! We need Trina to be awake so she can tell us who they are!"

"Yeah, she's been real forthcoming with that." Dover sneered.

Gabe pounded on the wall, accidentally hitting the black strip and sending a spray of brown liquid rocketing from a nearby nozzle. Dover jumped back, even though it wasn't really pointed at him. Gabe looked at the greasy brown liquid coursing down the tiles toward the drain and immediately dropped his fist.

"Look, if they catch up to us, and she's passed out, she'll be deadweight. You saw the way she drove—we need her to help us escape."

"And I'm saying *we won't need to escape from anyone* if we just leave her out of commission and put her back where she belongs," Dover said, as though speaking to a child or elderly person. "Do you even hear yourself? You're referring to her as 'awake' and 'passed out.' She's not a real girl, Gabe, she's a frigging robot, okay? She doesn't have thoughts, she doesn't have feelings, and *she doesn't care about you*!"

"I know what she is!" Gabe said. "My dad is the one who built her, remember?"

"Then why are you acting like she's your *girlfriend*? Would you risk our lives for a . . . for a car? Or for a laptop? NO! No, you frigging wouldn't! You're falling in love with her, and she's a *machine*! That's just pathetic! You're *pathetic*!"

"The hell with this—and the hell with you! I'm taking Trina home, and you can *walk* for all I care!" Gabe stormed out of the spray-tanning room and down the hall to the room where Trina was. If she was even partially charged, he'd be able to boot her up. He'd just make sure she conserved her energy by not moving around too much. Sort of like when his BlackBerry was about to die and he didn't make calls on it but sent brief texts. *See?* he said to himself as he pushed open the door to the tanning chamber. *I know she's not—*

"—here?" he said out loud. The tanning bed was open and empty. Trina's clothes were gone—and so was she.

Gabe whirled around in the doorway and collided with Dover.

"She's gone!" he pushed past Dover and out into the hall-way. He didn't want Dover to see how hurt he was.

"What? She must still be here, though—we'd have seen her go, right?"

"She might have gone out the front," Gabe called over his shoulder as he raced down the hallway toward the reception area.

"That guru guy would have stopped her! We haven't paid yet, and she doesn't have any money," Dover reminded him as he followed.

Gabe rounded the corner into the front room and came to

a halt, causing Dover to plow into him from behind. Rick was doing deep-knee bends in time with a curly-headed man on the video monitor.

"Make it burn, fatty!" shouted the man on TV.

"Good idea," Rick chuckled. "You boys wanna burn a fatty?" he said to Gabe and Dover, the muscles in his thighs rippling as he squatted deeply. "You look a little stressed out."

"Did you see Tr—Did my sister just come through here?" Gabe ignored the question.

"Sure did." Rick nodded toward the door. "She split about three minutes ago. Looked real good on the front side."

"But—but we didn't pay!" Gabe stuttered. "How could you let her go?"

"Like I said," Rick bent over to grasp his ankles as the over-zealous man on the TV screen did the same, "she reminded me of myself when I was her age. No biggie."

Gabe felt his vision blur with tears of frustration and shook his head. He couldn't let her get away! With Dover hot on his heels, he raced to the front door and looked outside. The Beavle was gone.

"Oh my God!" Gabe slammed his hands desperately against the glass. "The car is gone! We're screwed!"

Just then, a heavy hand descended on his shoulder.

"Yeah," a gravelly, masculine voice said. "You could say that."

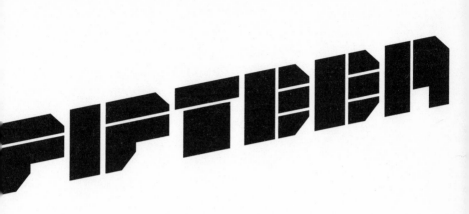

FIFTEEN

ALL TRUTHS ARE EASY TO UNDERSTAND ONCE THEY ARE DISCOVERED; THE POINT IS TO DISCOVER THEM.

—GALILEO GALILEI

GABE'S THROAT TIGHTENED. THE OWNER OF THE HAND PRO-pelled him and Dover forward out the door, into the parking lot, and around the corner. Gabe's heart sank at the sight of the black SUV idling. The blonde woman was at the wheel, and she smiled at the sight of them, which Gabe thought was weird and kind of scary. Her straight blond hair was darker than Trina's and pulled back in a ponytail, and her eyes looked lighter. A silky, cream-colored camisole peeked out from under her severe gray suit. Gabe would have described her as attractive . . . if he hadn't been so frightened of her.

The man opened the door behind her seat and shoved Gabe and Dover roughly inside. They landed hard on the floor, which was covered in scratchy, gray-black carpet. The backseats had been removed, leaving ample room for the man to climb in behind them and shut the door.

"Drive," he ordered the woman—but she was already peeling out of the parking lot. Gabe craned his neck, hoping to catch sight of the Beavle. A hand on his T-shirt jerked him around so that he was facing the gray-haired man. The man looked back and forth between Gabe and Dover; then he opened his jacket. Gabe sucked in his breath sharply as he took in the harness the man wore over his crisp white shirt: Just beneath his left armpit, in a brown leather holster, rode a wicked-looking gun—the gun he had used at the gas station to shoot at Gabe and Dover. Gabe saw Dover blanch, and his own vision blurred. Was the man going to kill them here and now?

But the man wasn't reaching for the gun. Instead, his hand came out gripping a small leather wallet. He unfolded it and held it up so Gabe and Dover could see it. It wasn't a wallet—it was a badge.

"NSA agent Roger Horton," the man announced, as Gabe and Dover read the words on his badge. "And that's Agent Kate Applewhite." He gestured toward the front seat. The blonde woman caught Gabe's eye in the rearview mirror and nodded slightly.

"With . . . with the National Security Agency?" Gabe asked.

"That's right." Agent Horton replaced his badge in his jacket pocket. "As you know," he looked squarely at Gabe, "your father was in charge of microelectromechanical systems and micro-optics at the NSA, designing and building extremely advanced robots to take the place of human spies."

As you know? Gabe tried as hard as he could not to let shock register on his face. Keeping his watery blue eyes locked resolutely on Agent Horton's steely gray ones, he listened intently, trying to tune out Dover's reaction, which was one of obvious and abject confusion. Gabe had figured out that Trina was no Amerivac creation . . . but the NSA? Was *that* why his dad was such a hard-ass about the basement lab?

"At approximately twenty hundred hours today," the agent continued, "the prototype went off temp base and has now been AWOL for exactly five hours and seventeen minutes. It is imperative that we retrieve the unit as soon as possible, and to that end we are hereby enlisting your aid."

He stopped talking, and the car fell absolutely silent. Then Dover erupted.

"Whaaaaaaat?" Color flooded into his face. "Wow, that's a good one." Dover pointed from Agent Horton to Agent Applewhite and back again. "Did Mack put you up to this? I mean, did he hire you?"

"I told you," Agent Horton said tightly, a vein pulsing faintly in his forehead. "I work for the NSA, as does Gabe's father. Market Access and Compliance is not in any way related to this project—at least as far as we know." He trained his gaze on Gabe. "But perhaps you'd know more about that."

"M-market Access and Compliance?" Gabe had no idea what this guy was talking about, and he really wished he did, because this guy had a *gun*.

"MAC, as your friend just mentioned. The government arm that deals with international trade compliance. *Trade* not being a word the NSA is anxious to hear in relation to Operation Butterfly."

"Operation *what?*" Gabe could no longer conceal his confusion.

"Butterfly," Horton snapped. "The program to create undetectable robotic spies. The one with the *missing prototype.*"

Holy. Shit. Gabe turned to look at Dover.

"Well," Dover said, "I guess I can't blame you for falling in love with her: If she was supposed to fool, like, government leaders, I guess a guy like you was a piece of cake."

Gabe turned bright red. "I am *not* in love with her!" he shouted. "And this is all your fault anyway! If you hadn't been bored three hours into your Friday night, we'd be home playing *Halo* like we always do instead of *at gunpoint* on the streets of some nameless suburb at one in the morning!"

"*You* were the one who broke into the lab!" Dover pointed out.

"You *made* me do it! Remember all that bullshit about how you helped me open the door so I wouldn't take the blame alone if I got into any trouble? Where's that guy now, huh? Oh, *I* know—he's been replaced by the dick who threw my phone out the window at a hundred miles an hour on the highway so my dad couldn't call me!

"And speaking of my dad," he continued, turning to Agent Horton, "I don't know what the hell you're talking about!

Yeah, he's an electromechanical engineer, but he's made *vacuum cleaners* for Amerivac since before I was born!"

"You don't know what I'm talking about?" Horton pushed his face in Gabe's. "Did you or did you not exit the premises of 329 Gilmore Avenue today—"

"Yesterday," Agent Applewhite said from the front seat.

"Yesterday at approximately twenty hundred hours in pursuit of a dangerous, top-secret, multimillion-dollar robot?"

Gabe blanched. *Dangerous? Multimillion-dollar?*

"Well, yeah, but we didn't know—"

"That robot is a *killing machine*!" Horton snarled. "It is imperative that we locate and deactivate it immediately!"

"Trina—Trina is a killing machine?" Dover gasped.

Agent Applewhite braked hard and fast, pulling over to the curb and sending the back area's three occupants flying against each other. Horton quickly regained his composure and lunged at Dover, gripping him by the front of his T-shirt.

"How do you know the acronym for the Truelife Robotic Intelligence New Assailant prototype?" Horton shouted. "There's no way you could know that unless—"

"I opened her up, all right?" Gabe interrupted. Horton stared.

"You *what*?" he asked in disbelief, releasing Dover's shirt.

"I opened her up." Gabe was relieved to finally be telling the story. "My parents went out of town for the weekend, and we decided to break into my dad's lab to see if there was any cool gear in there. We found Trina and . . ."

"And *what?*" Horton demanded.

Gabe snuck a glance at Dover. His friend looked just as guilty as he felt.

"We thought she was a sex robot," Dover broke in. "You know, like a blow-up doll, but way better."

Agent Applewhite snorted from the front seat. Horton looked shocked.

"So we, uh, took a look at her, and figured out how to access her hard—" Gabe stopped short. Maybe it wouldn't be such a good idea to let a couple of NSA agents know that he had managed to reprogram their spy robot with his and Dover's personalities. After all, they didn't need to know *everything*. "We, ah, figured out how to get her, um, little back panel off," he said lamely. "We saw her name was stamped on a piece of metal inside it, but that was all."

"That was all, huh?" Horton eyed Gabe suspiciously. "How did you boot her up?"

"She just seemed to power on when I put the panel back." Gabe went on to briefly outline Trina's departure, her reappearance at the gas station, and their detour to the party, leaving out the parts about kissing and undressing. ". . . and then she asked us if we could, uh, stop at the tanning salon, and that's when she ran away again," he finished, sweating slightly.

Horton was looking more relaxed now. He leaned against

the back of Applewhite's seat and looked thoughtfully at Gabe and Dover. They had begun driving again at some point while Gabe was talking. He looked out the window and realized they were about to get on the highway. *What the—?*

He didn't have a chance to form a sentence, though, because Horton was speaking.

"The 'sex robot' you think you found is a highly sophisticated robot that the NSA has been working on for years. Your father"—he nodded at Gabe—"is in charge of the project. Several months ago, he insisted on bringing Trina to his personal lab, so he could fine-tune her.

"I work for the NSA's internal affairs division, and I've been monitoring Milton since the project began. That's standard procedure," he added, as Gabe opened his mouth. "Or at least, it was in the beginning. I'm afraid your father has plans for Trina that involve larceny, espionage, and treason."

Gabe jerked forward. *What?*

Agent Applewhite spoke up from the front seat. "The NSA recently intercepted transmissions between one of its own operatives and a foreign power." She cast Gabe a sympathetic glance in the rearview mirror. "We have reason to believe that your father may be planning to sell the prototype to the North Korean government."

Gabe felt light-headed. "My dad? Are you kidding? He was in the army! He calls the school if the flag isn't out in the morning when he drops me off!"

Applewhite made a sympathetic noise as she signaled to change lanes.

"We learned, through telephone surveillance, that your parents were going out of town this weekend," Horton said, "which, as I'm sure you're aware, is a highly unusual occurrence. We thought that this meant that Milton might be making the transfer this weekend, and so we staked out your house. It became clear that Milton wasn't moving Trina himself, but we thought he might have arranged for a contact to make the pickup following his departure. We hadn't planned on her running away to escape two teenage sex maniacs," he finished, cracking a smile for the first time since they'd gotten in the car.

"We're not sex maniacs!" Gabe blushed hotly.

"Speak for yourself," Dover retorted. "Man, this is so messed up! Your dad is a corrupt NSA agent—that *totally* explains why he's such a dick!" He punched Gabe hard in the arm.

"He is *not*!" Gabe defended his father. "I mean, he may have built Trina for the NSA, but there's no way he's planning on selling her to the North Koreans!"

"Whatever the case," Horton stepped in, "we have to find Trina as soon as possible. The NSA isn't happy to hear that it has a forty-three-million-dollar killing machine on the loose."

Killing machine. Gabe went cold as he suddenly remembered the folder he'd been unable to access. The one that must have contained her deadly mission—the mission she was surely on now.

"Is . . . is she programmed to kill just anyone?" It couldn't be possible! She would have made mincemeat of him and Dover! Unless he had somehow overridden the drive by downloading their Facebook profiles into her constants, rendering her predisposed to like them?

"We don't know," Horton explained. "Milton was the last person to work with her—in fact, the *only* person to work with her for the last few months. That's why it's imperative we find her: We *just don't know* what he's programmed her to do. What she's capable of."

Gabe stared out the window at the darkness, broken only by the occasional blur of headlights of a car on the opposite side of the highway. He was beginning to wonder if he didn't know what his own father was capable of, either.

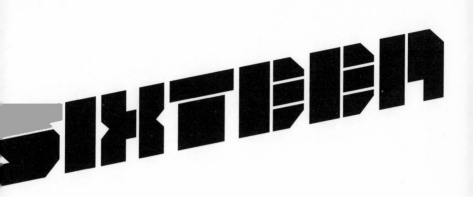

SIXTEEN

IT'S RIDICULOUS TO SET A DETECTIVE STORY IN NEW YORK CITY. NEW YORK CITY IS ITSELF A DETECTIVE STORY.

—AGATHA CHRISTIE

". . . PROBABLY GET GUYS HITTING ON YOU ALL THE TIME, HUH?"

Gabe awoke with a start. Where was he? Was Trina back? That was Dover's voice! Was he hitting on her?

Gabe pushed himself off the floor of the SUV and looked around. He must have fallen asleep pondering his father's supposed treasonous behavior the night before. Now the car was barreling into the sunrise, which revealed the skyline of . . . Gabe's bleary eyes focused on the unmistakable shape of the Empire State Building. *New York City!*

"Holy crap!" He scrambled to his knees and looked over the front seat. "What are we doing in New York?" He looked to his right. "And what are you doing in the front seat?"

"Just keeping Kate company," Dover said.

"*'Kate'?*"

"It was a long drive; he wore me down." The female agent looked tired. Faint purple shadows bloomed under her green eyes. But, Gabe had to admit, she was still very pretty. Of course, she was no Trina . . .

"We're approximately thirteen miles outside of New York City, on the approach to the George Washington Bridge,"

Horton announced. Gabe looked behind him to see the agent consulting a device that resembled a thinner, sleeker iPhone. "And to answer your question, we are tracking Trina and are hoping that this is her destination."

"And that she doesn't decide to continue on to, say, Boston." Kate laughed.

"Boston would be good with me." Dover leered at Kate. "I'll go *anywhere* with you!"

Kate rolled her eyes. "Is he always this bad?"

"Yes." All Gabe could think about was that single folder he'd been unable to access. *What was Trina programmed to do?* "How are you tracking her?" he asked Horton.

"LoJack," the agent said.

"What?" Gabe exclaimed.

"When we located you at the party, we searched your vehicle," Horton explained. "We found that it contained a LoJack tracking device. Normally, a car has to be reported stolen for the device to be activated. Owing to the top-secret nature of this case, we didn't want to get the local police involved, so we simply logged into the LoJack mainframe and activated the signal from there. That's how we found you at the tanning salon." He chuckled. "Not that you asked."

"But . . . don't you have to have a base unit to track the car?" Gabe's head was spinning.

Horton held up the slim device he'd been monitoring. "NSAM. NSA Multitracker. This provides secure access to the

NSA's intranet, from which I can download the necessary software for any tracking apparatus."

"Can you find an app that will make traffic go faster?" Kate asked. "The bridge is jammed."

Gabe was still thinking. "How did you log into LoJack in the first place?" he asked. "Isn't that a private company?"

"Yes," Horton said. "It is." Noting Gabe's confusion, he cracked a thin-lipped smile. "The NSA's ability to tap into LoJack is just the tip of the iceberg, thanks to sections two-oh-six and two-fifteen of the Patriot Act."

Just then, the NSAM emitted a high-pitched beeping sound. Gabe watched uneasily as Horton ran his fingers over the screen. The beeping stopped.

"What does that mean?"

"The car appears to have been in the same place for more than fifteen minutes, which means we can assume Trina has reached her destination," Horton explained.

Gabe felt a wave of emotions wash over him. He *really* wanted to see Trina again. The last time he'd seen her—well, the last time they'd had a conversation—she'd fallen asleep with her head on his shoulder. *Powered down*, he reminded himself. But what if he saw her again and she tried to kill him?

He stared out the window as the rocky outcroppings of upper Manhattan loomed. She couldn't be programmed to kill just anyone . . . she hadn't even come close to harming anyone in the hours they'd spent together. But what if she had been assigned a specific target and had just been using Gabe to reach it? Somehow that thought hurt most of all—even more than the idea that she might kill him.

Ugh. Gabe shut out all thoughts of his father programming a robot to kill and tried to remember Trina as she'd snuggled up to him in the backseat of the car. That was the Trina he was going to focus on. That was the Trina he wanted to see.

———— ————

Half an hour later, Gabe realized he might not be seeing Trina at all anytime soon. The SUV was only just coming off the bridge, and traffic was backed up down the Henry Hudson Parkway as far as the eye could see. What if Trina left before they got there?

"Do you think she'll still be . . . Where is she?" Gabe asked Horton. He'd spent the last ten minutes of the drive fruitlessly questioning Horton, trying to find out what the agent thought her mission was, or where he thought she might be. He had remained silent. Gabe was exasperated.

"According to LoJack, the car hasn't moved," said Horton. "She's parked at 1535 Broadway in Manhattan." He trained steel-gray eyes on Gabe. "You're going to have to be the one to approach her when we get there—she trusts you. We can't afford to lose sight of her again, so the question is, can *we* trust you?"

Gabe was taken aback. Of course they could trust him!

He opened his mouth to say as much and then thought for a moment about what might happen to Trina when they caught her. They would take her back to the lab, and he would never see her again. What if they took her apart? What if she was never *alive* again?

But then again, what if they *didn't* find her? It wasn't like she was going to be able to come back to his house. Even though Gabe didn't believe his dad was going to sell Trina to the North Koreans, it was possible *someone* might be trying to—Kate had said that someone in the NSA had contacted the North Korean government about a spy robot. And what if *no one* found her? Would she know where to go? What would happen when her solar power ran out again? He had made up his mind.

"Yeah." He met the older man's gaze. "You can trust me."

Horton nodded curtly at him. Then he reached out a hand. Gabe went to shake it but was thrown back against the door when the car took a sudden turn.

"Whoa!" Dover shouted. "Off-roading! Way to play, girl!"

"Sorry, everybody," Kate said over her shoulder as she steered the SUV onto a sharply angled exit. "We're still more than a hundred and thirty blocks from our destination, and the highway is packed, so I thought I'd take Broadway all the way down."

"Let me get coordinates for you." Dover reached for the GPS.

"That's okay," Kate said. "I went to college at Columbia, so I've got a pretty good grip on it, but thanks. That's the most gentlemanly offer you've made me all day."

Gabe rolled his eyes as Dover practically melted back into his seat. He turned to the window as the city flew by. For some reason, he found himself wishing Beverly were here. She would probably think all this tracking stuff was cool— although in *Lord of the Rings*, they didn't have, say, SUVs, GPSs, and NSAMs.

The SUV wended its way down Broadway, the scenery outside the windows giving way from grassy-hilled parks studded with rocks to bleak landscapes of boarded-up buildings and blowing trash, to brownstones. Kate pointed out places of interest as they passed, and Gabe tried to pay attention, because this *was* his first time in New York City. But mostly he felt fidgety and anxious.

"What's that building?" Dover asked as they passed a compound of poured-concrete buildings surrounding a sparkling fountain.

"That's Lincoln Center," Kate said. "Orchestras perform there. They have opera and ballet companies, too."

"Looks like a prime location for skateboarding," Dover observed.

"How much farther do we have left to go?" Gabe didn't really care about orchestras or skateboarding.

"About twenty blocks." Horton scanned the NSAM. "The cross street is Forty-fifth, and we're at Sixty-fourth now."

"Times Square!" Kate announced. "We'll be right underneath the Jumbotron. You guys are gonna love it!"

Gabe had to admit that Times Square was indeed amazing. Even though it was barely 8 A.M., the streets were filled with gawking tourists, shouting vendors, and a strange parade of characters in costume, including Spongebob SquarePants, Elmo, the Statue of Liberty, and a man who appeared to be naked save for a cowboy hat and a strategically placed acoustic guitar. He saluted Gabe and waved to the SUV as they passed. Gabe turned bright red and sank back into his seat.

"Whoa!" Dover exclaimed. "I'd much rather see a naked cow*girl*!"

As it turned out, they didn't get to park right beneath the glowing Jumbotron, because the SUV was diverted several blocks shy of Forty-fifth Street by a traffic cop who motioned them to turn right.

"Ugh." Kate spun the wheel. "They didn't have this pedestrian-plaza stuff when I was in school."

Portions of Broadway had been painted green and filled with lawn chairs; tourists had flopped down in many of them. In one chair sat a man wearing several layers of torn clothing, held onto his body with rope. A shopping cart was parked next to him, overflowing with garbage bags that appeared to be stuffed full of cans. It seemed like a weird place to relax to Gabe, but then, he reasoned, he'd seen hardly any grass in the last hundred blocks.

Finally they found a parking spot on the street—"A small victory!" exclaimed Kate—near Eleventh Avenue and Forty-fourth Street.

"It's too bad we don't have time to hang around." Kate looked much happier now that they were out of the SUV. "The *Intrepid* is docked just a block away."

"The what?" Dover said.

"The *Intrepid*," she explained. "It's a huge battleship from World War II. Now it's permanently docked here, but you can go on board and check it out. There's also a sub you can tour—it has nuclear missiles. Well, it fired nuclear missiles; I'm sure the ones on it now are disarmed," she said hastily, as Horton's expression darkened. "Anyway, it's pretty wicked. I wish we could go!"

Gabe cast a sidelong glance at Dover. He was gazing goo-goo-eyed at Kate. He felt a twinge of jealousy. He and Dover weren't really getting along at all, but Dover and Kate seemed to be doing just fine.

He shifted his thoughts back to Trina. He'd be seeing her soon . . . if they could even find her. The thought caused his heart to pound double time. What would he say to her? What would she say to him? Would she be happy to see him? Roger's words echoed in his head. Could Trina really be a kill-ing machine?

Horton interrupted his reverie and answered at least one of his unspoken questions.

"Ka—Agent Applewhite, Dover, and I are going to hang back," he instructed Gabe. "Specifically, we'll be just inside the entrance of the Marriott, waiting in the lobby, so we'll be able to see you the whole time, but Trina hopefully won't catch sight of us."

The four of them halted for a red light at the corner of Eighth Avenue and Forty-fifth Street, and Horton continued speaking as traffic whizzed by.

"You've logged the most time with the unit—with Trina," he amended, seeing the look on Gabe's face. "So you'll know what to say to her. But the important thing is that you get her powered down without anyone noticing."

Inside, Gabe felt only trepidation. Turning her off felt almost like . . . killing her. He had hated seeing her lose power at the party—and that had just been a result of drain. This time, he would be the one turning her off, not helping her. And then what? Would Horton take her back to the NSA? Would Gabe ever see her again? What if they wiped her memory and she didn't recognize him?

A large, red double-decker bus roared by. Kids waved happily from the top. Maybe if he could show Horton that Trina wasn't dangerous, he wouldn't need to power her down. What if she *was* dangerous? He still didn't want her to be destroyed. He decided he would go along as far as necessary. Even if he did have to power her down, maybe he could ride with her to NSA headquarters and talk to the tech team there about reprogramming her. Surely the fact that his dad built her would lend his case merit.

The light changed. Horton stepped off the curb.

"You'll have to find a way to steer her over toward the hotel entrance," he said to Gabe. "When you get close to the doors, put your hand on her back as though to guide her through—but press the power switch firmly. Agent Apple-white and I will meet you on the other side to catch her, so that she doesn't hit the floor and draw attention. Can you do that?" he asked, halting on the sidewalk and taking Gabe by the shoulders.

"Tourists!" an elderly man in a flak jacket and a Panama hat shouted from behind as he swerved to avoid them. Gabe ignored him.

"I can do it," Gabe said. Horton released him and clapped him on the back. Gabe felt a strange swelling of pride: This man, an NSA agent, trusted him. *Unlike my dad,* Gabe thought sadly. What was his dad doing right now? Did he wonder where Gabe was?

"All right, let's break!" Motioning to Kate and Dover, Horton veered off to the right as they approached Broadway. The three of them rounded the corner while Gabe kept going straight ahead. When he reached the corner, he looked across the street—and there it was: the Beavle.

Its springy, pale-green color looked out of place in the oversaturated neon glow of Times Square, even during the day. Gabe noticed, too, that there were no other cars on the side of the street on which it was parked. That was odd.

His heart in his throat, Gabe approached the little car. He would act carefree, breezy, as though it were a natural, everyday occurrence that he should run into a sexy robot that he knew intimately in New York City's Times Square.

"Hey," he stepped around to the driver's side window. "Fancy meeting you he—" He stopped and stared in at the smooth gray fabric of the driver's seat.

The car was empty.

Trina was gone.

SPYEA-
TUER

HE THAT KNOWS HIMSELF KNOWS OTHERS.

—CHARLES COLTON

GABE STEPPED BACK FROM THE CAR, HIS MIND REELING. *WHERE was Trina?* He gazed downtown at the flickering Jumbotron, the converging streams of honking traffic. Then he looked uptown, at the bright-red TKTS booth, its glowing stairs crowded with old people and eager students.

He shook his head. Why had they thought she would still be in the car anyway? What kind of healthy, red-blooded girl—or decently programmed robot, for that matter—would drive a car all the way to Times Square just to hang out in it? Maybe she was nearby doing some shopping? After all, he *had* programmed her to like Victoria's Secret.

Gabe made his way to the Marriott hotel. Horton was right: Trina wouldn't have been able to see inside. But Horton could certainly see out—he was through the glass door and upon Gabe practically before Gabe's feet left the street and hit the sidewalk's curb.

"Where is she?" he shouted, red-faced. "WHERE IS SHE?!"

Gabe was taken aback. He had thought they were getting along. It wasn't like *he* wanted Trina to be missing either. What was this guy's damage?

Kate and Dover came spilling out of the revolving door in the hotel's center.

"Wow, this chick is the Energizer bunny!" Dover said. "She just keeps going and going and going." He looked speculatively at Gabe. "She must have been really something in the sack, huh?"

Gabe was about to issue a hot retort to his horny friend, but Dover noticed Horton's face and clammed up.

"We now have the unenviable task of searching for the unit in a city of more than eight million people," Horton raged. "If I find out you're holding out on me regarding her mission, so help me God . . ."

Kate put a calming hand on his arm. "Roger, we already went through this, remember?"

Horton stared at the ground for a long moment, and then appeared to regain control of himself.

"I apologize." He addressed Gabe. "I know you understand how important it is that we find Trina." He gazed out at the Beavle, which now had a bright orange ticket on its windshield, and then continued. "Since we don't have any idea what her mission is, we're going to have to reassess our own mission."

Gabe was stunned. Was he ready to give up on finding Trina? What would happen to her if they never found her?

"Um . . ." Dover looked meaningfully at Gabe. Gabe gulped, then steeled himself.

"Remember when I told you how we opened Trina up and saw her name on a piece of metal inside?" he asked Horton. The agent stiffened but nodded.

"Well, that isn't exactly all we saw," Gabe said. "We—I opened up her hard drive and . . . and did some reprogramming." He shifted nervously from foot to foot. "Because we thought she was a sex robot, we figured we ought to make her like us, so I programmed her to like stuff that we both like"— he gestured to Dover. "So . . . maybe if we go to the kinds of places we like . . . we could find her?"

Horton was staring at him with a mixture of fury and admiration. "How old are you?"

"Fifteen," said Gabe. What did *that* have to do with anything?

"Practically sixteen," hastened Dover, addressing Kate. The junior agent snorted.

"Is there anything else you'd like to tell me?" said Horton, rubbing the back of his neck. "Anything you 'accidentally' left out?"

"It's okay, Gabe. You couldn't have been expected to trust us entirely after the way we met." Kate gave a small laugh, and Gabe immediately felt the knot in his stomach loosen up.

"There *is* one more thing," he said. "I couldn't access her mission drive. I mean, I *think* it was her mission drive," he amended. "There was one folder I couldn't open."

"Well, that's a relief," Horton said with a wry smile.

"Upon learning she wasn't a sex robot, you might have reprogrammed her to become one."

"Oh, DUDE!" Dover wailed. Gabe willed himself not to blush. He hadn't thought of that!

"All right." Horton was all business again. "Where would Trina go . . . if she were a fifteen-year-old boy?"

——— ———

"Phew!" Dover said as he climbed out of the SUV four hours later. "I *never* thought I would get sick of comic book stores!"

"Tell me about it," Gabe agreed, surveying their surroundings. They were somewhere in Chinatown, having been to every comic book store in Manhattan. At first it had been exciting, going everywhere from Jim Hanley's Universe, where the best comic-book writers and artists, famous and cutting-edge, often held signings or readings, to the funky, basement-y St. Mark's Comics in the East Village.

But there had been no sign of Trina, and the hours of sitting in heavy traffic had taken their toll. Dover had perked up at Forbidden Planet, which had a special room devoted to anime porn, but his excitement had been squelched by a zit-faced boy wearing a Wolverine T-shirt and a name tag that identified him as ADAM ANTIUM. He had pointed sternly to a sign reading 18 AND OVER and hustled Dover away into the Pokémon section.

Now, fresh off a stop at a dark and crowded video game

parlor on Mott Street (*"Tekken 6!"* Gabe had exclaimed wistfully. "If Trina were here, this place would be perfect!"), they were about to enter the only comic book store in Manhattan they hadn't yet visited: Dragon Comics.

"Dragon has been at the top of my fantasy list for years," Gabe said as they climbed the chipped concrete steps to the little shop. "If she didn't come here, I think we can safely say that something went wrong during the profile download."

"I dunno. I kind of gave up hope when she wasn't at the arcade throwing down at *DDR*."

Gabe paused with his hand on the door. *"DDR?"*

"Dance Dance Revolution." Dover blushed. "You know, that old Konami game that's sort of like the dance version of *Guitar Hero*? I've always wanted to try it."

"Wow." Gabe shook his head as he yanked open the door. "You are one sick *otaku*. I think I liked it better when I just knew about your porn problem."

A little bell jingled as the door shut behind them. It was hidden by a tiny, traditional red-paper Chinese lantern, trimmed in gold. The store was small, but it was crammed almost to the ceiling with all the latest releases, several of which were being inspected intently by hoodie-wearing customers. Neat labels on long boxes jammed side by side beneath the racks announced their contents as being vintage or out-of-print comics; the back wall held graphic novels. Squinting, Gabe could make out several obscure titles he had long wanted to lay his hands on. Sure, he could get any one of them he wanted online—if he had hundreds of dollars to spend. But here he could just browse through them, hold them, and inspect them. He sighed, wishing he could spend more than three minutes here.

An impatient honk outside jolted him. He made his way toward the counter, which was elaborately shaped and painted like the head of a Chinese dragon. It was a little faded and scuffed, but still pretty badass. Behind it sat a plump, long-haired man in his early twenties. He wore glasses with thick black frames and a T-shirt with an illegible logo that looked liked it was made out of thorns. He was eating cheese crackers from a baggie.

"Excuse me," Gabe said to the clerk. "Have you seen a girl in here today?"

The man laughed. Confused, Gabe continued. "Blonde? About so tall"—he held his hand slightly above his own head—"busty, wearing kind of a short dress with flowers on it?"

"Kid." The clerk leaned forward, sending orange crumbs showering onto the dragon-head counter. "Look around you."

Gabe glanced around the shop. The only thing he saw that he hadn't noticed before was a shelf of toys, way up high, where he guessed customers weren't supposed to be able to reach them. He returned his gaze to the clerk, who spoke again, shaking his head.

"We haven't had a chick like that in here—*ever*. But . . ." He leaned back in his chair, put the empty baggie to his mouth, and blew into it, inflating it like a balloon. Then, with a loud crack, he popped it, sending crumbs flying. ". . . if you can get one in here, I'll give you a twenty percent discount on all the comics you can carry."

"Uh, that's okay. But thank you." Gabe turned and headed for the door.

"You gotta let me take pictures, though," the man called after him. "For the blog!"

"Damn," Dover said as they hustled down the stairs. "Now what?"

Horton echoed the same sentiment when they approached the SUV.

"So much for that great idea," he glared at Gabe as the two boys clambered into the back of the vehicle.

Gabe felt a momentary flash of anger. He was getting tired of Horton's bad-cop routine. It wasn't like any of this was his fault! And he and Dover had been doing all the legwork. He opened his mouth to say as much, but the agent went on.

"Since it seems that you failed in your download of data to the unit, we have to assume that it—that she is carrying out the function for which she was originally programmed," said Horton. "Since we're not certain what that function is, we need to look at what we know—which is that she is a killing machine, and that Milton Messner is planning on selling her to the North Korean government."

"Hey!" Gabe grabbed the back of the front seat as Kate pulled away from the curb. He thought of Trina resting her head on his shoulder, wistfully telling him how much she liked being around people. "We don't *know* that! In fact"—he banged on the headrest—"how do you even know she's a killing machine? You said yourself no one at the NSA but my dad has had access to her for months. She could be programmed to save lives for all you know!"

Horton shook his head adamantly. "No. The whole purpose behind this program—the reason the government spared no expense—is to create the world's most alluring killer. Yes, she can do spy duty, and yes, she can function in other capacities, but she is first and foremost a destructive agent. She was created *specifically* to kill."

Gabe's ears began to ring faintly. He focused on the silvery NSA logo of Kate's badge reflected in the windshield. The inside of the SUV had that rubbery, new-car smell. "You haven't spent any time with her. You don't know what she's really like," he said hotly. "And as for my dad selling her to the North Koreans, he's no traitor!"

"And how do *you* know *that*?" Horton countered. "Until this morning, you thought he had a job making vacuum cleaners!"

"ENOUGH!" Kate shouted from the driver's seat. "I think we can all safely agree that none of us knows what her mission is, or who is planning on selling her to North Korea. What we do know is that the North Korean government *is* interested in buying her, and that she was programmed to come to New York City. Now we have to figure out how those two things are connected." She braked to a sudden stop, swore, and then leaned on the horn.

"Um, where are we going?" Dover asked.

"Back to Midtown," Horton said tightly.

"I thought we decided we didn't need to stake out the car," Gabe said, "since the LoJack would show us if it started moving."

"Agent Applewhite and I decided we should search the vehicle to see if it can provide any clues as to where Trina may have gone," Horton said.

"If we ever get to it, that is," Kate said. "I've never seen traffic like this!"

Gabe looked ahead of them. Traffic was snarled tightly all around them. Frustrated drivers honked furiously at other drivers who were clearly trapped. A man got out of the back of a yellow cab and walked away. The cabbie yanked his cell phone headset from his mouth and shouted angrily after him.

"It wasn't like this when we came down here," Gabe said. "And it's way too early to be rush hour."

"It's Saturday," Dover pointed out, "so there wouldn't be rush hour anyway. Maybe we could turn on the radio and find out what's going on?" he suggested.

Kate reached over and flicked the radio on, pushing the STATION FIND button until she came to a crackly male voice.

". . . traffic report. Major delays on all inbound bridges and tunnels, and an accident taking up three lanes on the eastbound LIE," intoned the voice. "Drivers in Manhattan will want to avoid the East Side above Fourteenth Street, as the president's visit to the UN has surrounding streets and avenues shut down and traffic is heavy."

"Well," Gabe said, "that expla—" He stopped, seeing Kate's face. She had gone deathly pale, and her knuckles gripping the steering wheel were white.

"What? What is it?" Gabe swiveled his head around.

"The president," Kate said in a terrified voice. *"Trina's going to kill the president!"*

EIGHT- TEEN

TAKE A CHANCE! ALL LIFE IS A CHANCE! THE MAN WHO GOES FARTHEST IS GENERALLY THE ONE WHO IS WILLING TO DO AND DARE.

—DALE CARNEGIE

CARS, TRUCKS, AND BUSES JAMMED EVERY STREET AND AVENUE on the East Side. The mood in the SUV was tense: Kate gripped the wheel and stared stoically ahead, while Horton fumed next to her, tapping his hand relentlessly against the cupholder separating the two seats. In back, Dover and Gabe were silent as the low storefronts of Allen Street gave way to the stark high-rises of First Avenue. An ambulance siren wailed blocks behind them.

Gabe couldn't stop thinking about his father. Why would he want to kill the president? It was true that he hadn't voted for him, but Gabe had even overheard him grudgingly admit to Gloria that he felt the president was unexpectedly doing certain things right. Then Gabe thought of all the things he had learned that day: that his father worked for the NSA, and that he was capable of constructing a robot that walked, talked, and looked like the world's most beautiful woman—*in his house*, without his *entire family* knowing about it. But he couldn't be a traitor! He just couldn't be!

"So . . ." Gabe finally spoke. "What's our plan when we get to the UN?"

"At this rate, we won't be able to reach the president's entourage before speech time. We're going to have to go directly to the General Assembly Hall," said Kate, looking at the digital clock on the dash. "If we're lucky, we should get there just before the president begins speaking. Hopefully we'll be able to spot Trina in the audience; the hall has excellent sight lines."

Next to her, Horton shifted and checked the NSAM's LoJack tracker, as he'd done incessantly for the past hour. Peering over his shoulder, Gabe could see that the vehicle hadn't moved. It seemed amazing to him that it hadn't been towed. Touching the NSAM's screen again, Horton brought up a photo of the hall's interior and then scrolled to a floor plan.

"We'll have to spread out upon entering the auditorium," he said. "Although we know she's programmed to kill, we don't know her method. She may have a gun or a knife . . . or she may have no implement."

"Y-you mean she'd use her bare hands?" Gabe stammered.

Horton nodded. "If she could get close enough to him fast enough, she could break his neck or strangle him. I'd assume the former as it takes less time."

Gabe felt sick. He'd known Trina for less than twenty-four hours, but he just couldn't believe she'd do something like that. He tried to block out the memories of her sticking up for him when Dover threw his BlackBerry out the window, of her hand in his, of her kiss—but it was hard.

"Keep in mind," Horton said, almost as though he were reading Gabe's thoughts, "one of the reasons she's as beautiful as she is, is to make it easier for her to get close to her target."

Gabe winced. Had *he* been her target? Had she used him?

"Wow, beautiful but deadly." Dover tried to catch Kate's eye in the rearview mirror. "That's . . . actually kinda hot."

Horton ignored him. "Agent Applewhite will take the left rear of the hall. Dover, you'll take the right rear. I'll take the front, nearest the lectern. Gabe, you'll need to be in the middle, to act as a free agent. We'll figure out which side you'll be on when we get there."

"A free agent?" Gabe was confused.

"Trina knows and likes you," Kate explained. "Seeing you might momentarily distract her. We need you to be able to assist whoever takes her down."

Whoever takes her down. Gabe couldn't believe this was happening.

"Are . . . I mean, I know she's a robot, but are we going to kill her? Or destroy her, or whatever?"

"As I said before, Trina is a forty-three-million-dollar machine," Horton said. "The NSA would prefer her to come to as little harm as possible. Obviously, our first mission is to protect the president, but it would be preferable if we could do so without injuring Trina."

Kate addressed Gabe. "Thanks to her power switch, we can stop her without harming her in some way."

Gabe felt a little better. Then he remembered the way Trina's head had drooped when she was losing power. She had seemed so sad, like she hated to leave. He didn't want to make her feel that way again! He hoped the switch was wired for abrupt power-off.

"Okay." Kate maneuvered into a tight parking space between a motorcycle and an old Volkswagen bus covered with green glitter, "I think this is as close as we're going to be able to get and still get there before the president speaks. We'll just have to walk from here."

Dover and Gabe exited quickly through the rear doors, while Agent Horton walked around the front of the car, fishing in his pocket for quarters, which he handed to Kate.

"I hope we can get this done in"—Kate squinted at the meter—"two hours," she said as she fed the coins into the slot. "Otherwise Trina will wind up costing just a little bit more than forty-three million dollars."

Despite her joking tone, Gabe could see that Kate was nervous. Her lips were pressed together tightly, and the carefree attitude she'd displayed earlier in the afternoon was gone. Even Dover was antsy, hopping from one foot to the other as Kate checked to see that the SUV was locked.

The quartet hurried up First Avenue and over the little bridge at Forty-second Street. The United Nations loomed before them, its glassy face appearing almost aqua in the sun. Guards in dark-blue uniforms dotted the concrete walkway.

Farther beyond, to the north, lay the sculpture garden, with its lush green grass and trees just beginning to flower.

"Whoa," Dover said. "I hope you guys know your way around this place."

Horton pointed at a long, much lower concrete building with a dome rising from the middle. "That's the General Assembly Hall. We'll be accessing it from the Secretariat Building, though." He nodded at the taller building.

The four made their way to the main entrance, passing under the flags that ringed the complex as they did so. Gabe looked up in awe; he wished they were here under different circumstances. There was so much he wanted to see! He had read that the UN even had its own post office. How cool was that?

They approached the glass doors. Numerous security guards stood on the other side. A man in a sleekly tailored suit was removing his watch as he prepared to enter the metal detector. Gabe had an idea.

"Hey," he said, "wouldn't Trina have set off the metal detector? Since she's a robot and all?"

Horton shook his head. "The compound alloys used in her construction are undetectable by normal metal-sensing devices. She needs to be able to fly out of any airport in the world, if necessary."

He opened the door and the group filed in. A tall security guard approached them.

"May I see your identification, please?" he asked. Kate held up her badge. The guard inspected it closely and waved her through. Horton went through the same process. Then it was Gabe's turn. Too late, he realized his and Dover's predicament: They didn't even have learners' permits, let alone licenses. What was Dover going to show them—his school ID?

"Um," he dug in the pockets of his jeans, "I seem to have misplaced my identification." He smiled winningly at the guard. "Of course you understand."

The guard shook his head. "No ID, no entrance."

Gabe looked ahead. Horton and Kate had placed their guns in a plastic bin and were about to enter the metal detector, completely unaware of the events unfolding behind them. Then he looked at the old-fashioned clock on the huge rotunda; the president was due to speak in just seven minutes! He had to think fast. Casting a meaningful glance at Dover, he turned back to the guard.

"Listen, this is Do'Vair Mik'Elson, the delegate from French Antigua. I am . . . filling in for his translator at the last minute. Mr. Mik'Elson is scheduled to attend the U.S. president's speech in just minutes. It is imperative that you let us through."

The guard remained resolute. "Youth delegates are not permitted at this function. I'm afraid I'll have to ask you to leave."

Gabe opened his mouth to speak but was interrupted by a torrent of words from behind him.

"Comment ossez-vous?" Dover demanded, drawing himself up to his full height. Despite his raggedy corduroys, he managed to convey a dignity and rage Gabe had never known him to be capable of. *"Vous me prendriez pour un enfant? Je suis un véritable diplomate représentant l'Antigua français!"*

The guard's brow wrinkled in confusion. Silently, Gabe thanked Dover's parents and his own for making them take French since junior high.

"He says he is outraged that you have mistaken him for a child," Gabe explained, "and that he is a full-fledged diplomat representing the island nation of French Antigua."

Dover began to shout, waving his arms in fury.

"It is outrageous that an employee of the United Nations responsible for the protection of denizens of all nations does not know that the people of French Antigua are of comparatively diminutive size and youthful appearance," Gabe translated. "Never in all his thirty-three years has the esteemed delegate been treated thusly."

Dover gestured forcefully to Kate and Horton, who were picking up their weapons from the other side of the metal detector and were only now becoming aware of Gabe and Dover's predicament.

"It is a further affront to Ambassador Mik'Elson that you let his bodyguards, operatives of your own country's National

Security Agency, past without so much as a murmur while he, who has risked his life in order to serve a nation so recently thrown into a state of emergency, is held at the gate like a common teenager off the street." Gabe took a deep breath as Dover continued yelling. "He demands to know if you want an international incident on your hands! He—"

"Sir, please, enough!" the beleaguered guard cut in, as Horton and Kate approached, frowning. "I apologize for the inconvenience. Please . . ." He motioned Gabe and Dover toward the metal detector.

Immediately, Dover calmed down, assuming the demeanor befitting a dignitary. Gabe, remembering his role as "translator," motioned his "boss" to go first.

"*Merci, mon ami.*" Dover clapped the guard on the shoulder as he passed. "*Vous êtes un homme bon. J'essayerai d'oublier cet incident, pour la paix internationale.*"

"He says you're a good man," Gabe picked up his pace as he passed the guard, lest he change his mind, "and that he is willing to put the incident behind him for the sake of international peace."

"Thank you, sir," the guard called after him.

Kate and Horton, upon seeing the boys let through, immediately bolted for the auditorium. Gabe didn't have time to think about whether or not it looked weird that they were abandoning their "charge," because before he knew it, he was through the metal detector and free to go.

"YES!" Dover held up his hand for a high five. Gabe smacked it violently.

"Did you *see* that guy's face? When you told him I was thirty-three years old?"

"Did you see Horton's face when I said he was your body-guard?" Gabe doubled over in hysterics.

"Priceless!" Dover agreed through tears of laughter. "And French Antigua? Where is that, anyway?"

"I made it up!" Gabe gasped. "I thought, what if I name some country and the guy was just here? I mean, what representative is going to skip the president's . . ." He trailed off. *The president!* He looked at the clock. It was almost three. They had less than thirty seconds!

"Come on!" he shouted to Dover, and the two friends took off running in a fashion most unsuited to a dignitary and his translator. They pounded down a long, glossy-floored hallway, and caught up with Horton and Kate just as they were entering the General Assembly Hall.

"Nice work." Kate gave them both a quick smile.

"Damn," Horton hissed. "There's no chance to spread out before the president gets onstage. We're just going to have to take it from here."

Gabe looked out over the domed auditorium, with its muted green carpet and curving, wood-paneled walls. A swooping feeling rushed through his stomach. *Holy crap!* Yesterday, he'd been tossed in a Dumpster by the school bully:

Now he was in New York City, in the United Nations frigging General Assembly Hall about to see the president of the United States speak!

A hush fell over the auditorium. Gabe looked around. Everyone was focused on the stage. Even the guards stationed near the front seemed excited. Then the president walked out. The audience rose, and Gabe remembered his mission. *Trina!* Frantically, he scanned the crowd. Lots of suits and short hair . . . and then . . .

As the president took his spot at the lectern in front of the golden wall with the United Nations symbol on it, the audience took their seats, and Gabe spotted a flash of long, platinum-blonde hair. His heart fluttered—and then sank. Horton had been right. His father had programmed Trina to kill the president. His father was a traitor. And the girl—the *robot*—he'd made out with was a *killer*. He knew what he had to do.

"There!" he hissed to Kate, who was nearest him. She stiffened and followed his gaze. The president began to speak, and the blonde woman shifted slightly in her seat. Gabe cast an agonized glance at Horton and Dover, who had moved to the other side of the back of the auditorium, but they were intently scrutinizing attendees in their section and didn't see him. He returned his gaze to the blonde woman. Her back was to him, and she was wearing a tight, dark-blue suit, not the flowered dress she'd worn when he'd last seen her, but that was Trina. He was sure of it!

Kate seemed sure of it, too. Slowly, with an almost eerie calm, she reached for her gun. Gabe gulped as the weapon emerged from its holster. He had hoped they wouldn't have to hurt Trina, but she was so far away. Could he get to her in time, before she got to the president—and before Kate had to shoot her? He looked over at Kate, but she shook her head at him ever so slightly, as if reading his thoughts.

How had this gone so wrong? he wondered. He wished he could will Trina to look at him—*yes*, she was a robot, but they'd had a connection! If she would just look at him, maybe she would forget her mission, or maybe she would hesitate long enough that Kate wouldn't shoot her and he could get her out of here somehow.

The woman leaned forward. Gabe was squarely behind her, so he couldn't tell what she was doing, but it looked like she was rummaging through her purse. She brought a hand up. Gabe heard Kate cock the safety on the gun. *Oh, God!* And then, as if in slow motion, the woman turned to look at him . . .

. . . and she wasn't Trina.

NINE-
TEEN

FROM ERROR TO ERROR, ONE DISCOVERS THE
ENTIRE TRUTH.

—SIGMUND FREUD

GABE PRACTICALLY MELTED INTO THE REAR WALL OF THE AUDITO-rium. Next to him, he heard Kate let out a shaky breath as she lowered her gun. The blonde woman lifted up a small compact and, peering into its tiny mirror, began to powder her nose. Gabe had to cover his mouth to keep from laughing. The woman he had thought was a beautiful spy robot hefting a Glock 9mm was in fact a middle-aged woman fixing her makeup.

Despite his relief, Gabe felt a slight pang of sadness. He was starting to wonder if he would ever see Trina again. They had been searching for her since late last night, and he realized that he had never considered the possibility that they might not find her. Of course, he would rather it not be under these circumstances, but still . . .

Horton and Dover, who had finally noticed his and Kate's distress, came running over.

"What's going on?" Horton asked. Kate briefly explained the case of mistaken identity, while Gabe joined Dover in surveying the audience.

"All right," Horton whispered. "We're going to stay till

the end of the speech. Just because we haven't seen her yet doesn't mean she isn't here."

———— ————

An hour later, as the president wrapped up his speech and left the podium without a scratch on him, it became evident that Trina was not, in fact, in the UN General Assembly Hall. Horton motioned Kate, Gabe, and Dover toward the exits as the attendees rose and began to make their way out. Gabe was feeling exhilarated.

"So," he said to no one in particular as the group strolled down the walkway in front of the UN at a much more leisurely pace than that at which they had run up it, "it doesn't look like my dad programmed Trina to kill the president, does it?"

"I'm glad we were wrong." Kate smiled at him as they approached the end of the broad concrete walk leading to First Avenue. She looked visibly relaxed, and the sparkle had returned to her green eyes.

"I'm glad I got to see you take your gun out." Dover leered good-naturedly at Kate. "Now I can replay it over and over in my mind instead of just fantasizing about it. God, it was hot."

He turned to Gabe. "Your dad may be a dick," he said, "but I never *really* thought he wanted to kill the president."

Gabe grinned back at his best friend. He was still mad that he had thrown his BlackBerry from a moving vehicle—and he really hoped Milton didn't have a stroke because of it—but at least Dover seemed to be acting more like his old self again. Gabe lifted his hand, and Dover smacked it.

Horton looked sour. "You two can high-five all you want, but Trina is still missing, and killing is still her mission. Milton may have programmed her to go after an equally unthinkable target."

"It's kind of looking like he programmed her to drive you *insane!*" Dover said. Horton knitted his brows but said nothing.

"Speaking of insane," Kate said as they approached the Forty-second Street bridge, "traffic already seems less crazy than when we drove up here."

"Yeah," Gabe agreed, speaking loudly to be heard over the roar of a passing city bus, "at least it's mov—"

He halted. The bus was pulling into the stop across from them. It was a double bus, with an accordionlike fold in the middle, and the vehicle's rear half was plastered with an advertisement for Dr. Phil's television show. According to the word balloon protruding from Dr. Phil's airbrushed, crazy-looking mouth, the show was on "every afternoon at 4:00!!!!"

Gabe felt as though the sky had opened up and a beam of light was pouring down upon him. *Of course!*

"I know what it is!" he shouted, whirling to face the others. "Trina is programmed to *kill Dr. Phil!*"

Horton, Kate, and Dover stared at him.

Dover spoke first, his eyes wide. "Do you really think your dad hates him that much?"

"Oh my God, *yes*! Remember when my mom cut off our Wi-Fi and hid my dad's BlackBerry? And how mad my dad was?"

"Boy, do I ever," said Dover. "I think you must have slept over at my house every night for a week."

"That's because she saw on his show that you were supposed to do that to improve your marriage. And the personality test, do you remember that? She decided he had a 'porcupine' personality and that she had a 'Chicken Little' personality, and he blew up and said they weren't zoo animals?"

Dover nodded. "But aren't your parents on some kind of Dr. Phil retreat right now? Wouldn't Trina be *there* if she were programmed to kill him?"

"They're on a Dr. Phil–*approved* retreat. Some place he mentioned on his show where you get back to nature and, I don't know, live in a tent and pretend the electric can opener was never invented," Gabe said. "But he's not actually *at* the retreat. If he was, my dad definitely wouldn't have gone."

"A *television show host*?" Horton was incredulous. "Milton Messner would build a sophisticated, beautiful machine like Trina and then waste it—her—on some idiot TV personality? I don't believe it!"

"Hey, that's what *I* said when you said my dad programmed her to kill the president," Gabe pointed out, "but we followed up on that lead. And *this* one is much more informed!"

"All right, all right. Let's see if this is even a viable option— if Dr. Phil is even in the area." Kate whipped an NSAM identical to Horton's from her jacket pocket and tapped on its face. "Oh my God!" she exclaimed after a few seconds. "He's doing a book signing at the Barnes & Noble in *Times Square!*" She looked at the phone again. "*In twenty minutes!*"

Even Horton looked shaken. "All right." He spread his hands. "Let's go!"

The four raced down the few blocks of First Avenue remaining between them and the car. Kate backed up and peeled out, burning rubber as she guided the SUV up the avenue, back toward Forty-second Street.

"Did you see that?" she crowed. "And with time to spare on the meter!"

Horton made a fast check of the NSAM. "The car is still there," he shook his head. "I wonder where she's been all this time."

"Victoria's Secret?" Dover suggested. "I saw one on the way down. We added the catalog to her profile," he said a bit guiltily.

"WHAT?" Horton turned around in his seat. "She could have been in a store just *blocks* from where she originally parked all morning and you somehow neglected to mention this possibility?"

"I didn't think it *was* a possibility," Dover yelled back, "since both of us hate shopping!" He gestured to Gabe.

"There's no point in arguing about where she might have been." Kate turned onto Forty-second Street. "What we need to focus on now is getting to the Barnes & Noble and finding her before she finds Dr. Phil!"

"I can't believe your dad actually programmed her to kill Dr. Phil," Dover said.

"What do you mean, you can't believe it?" Gabe snapped. "You were ready to believe he programmed her to kill the *president*!" He stared out the window. It was mid-afternoon now, and he was kind of wishing they'd gotten to stop for a slice of pizza or something before he saw the bus and got the idea about Dr. Phil. But then, he reminded himself, he would have been getting the idea too late. Too late for Dr. Phil. Would he really be . . . dead?

"I just mean, I know your mom drives him crazy with watching Dr. Phil and talking about the show . . . and acting on his advice all the time," Dover admitted, "but going so far as to have the guy killed? Also, I don't get what this would have to do with the North Koreans. Why would they want a robot programmed to kill a cheesy psychologist?"

"It's not who the robot is programmed to kill," Horton replied before Gabe could speak. "It's that the robot *can* be programmed to kill. That's what makes Trina potentially worth billions of dollars to any power." He got a faraway look in his eyes.

Ew, Gabe thought. Was he imagining Trina killing someone? Gabe felt a familiar pang of possessiveness, but then remembered Dover's question.

"I don't think my dad would really have done that," he said. "I mean, I think he *did* do that, but, like, as a joke—you know, as a placeholder, thinking he'd erase it or replace it when he returned her to the NSA. You know," he appealed to Dover, "like when you have to write a paper for school and you're mad about it or whatever, so you start the paper 'When I grow up, the last thing I am going to do with my life is become a bitch-ass English comp teacher at Roosevelt High.' And then you delete it before you actually write the rest of the paper or before you turn it in."

"Yeah," Dover said, "I guess I do know what you mean. I started a paper for physics class with an analysis of Ms. Favreau's cup size and forgot to take that paragraph out."

"An analysis?"

"Well, an educated guess based on mass. I'm pretty sure I was right, though. Still," he mused, "it seems awfully dangerous."

Gabe bristled. "I guess so. I still don't see how he could have predicted any of this happening." In a way, though, he *had* predicted almost all of it, Gabe thought. Milton had contrived an elaborate security system to keep anyone from getting into the lab. Then he'd dressed Trina as a maid, so that if someone *did* breach the system and find her, they'd think she was just a domestic droid. The only thing Milton hadn't planned on, it appeared, was Gabe reprogramming his creation. The thought made Gabe strangely proud.

"All right," Kate said, "we're coming up on Times Square. Everybody keep an eye out for parking."

Gabe looked out the window. This time, he was entering

Times Square from the south. There were even more people thronging its streets than there had been this morning. He looked up. High overhead, news headlines scrolled in LED lights across a tall, slender white chip of a building. PRESIDENT CONCLUDES SPEECH AT U.N. TORNADOES RIP THROUGH MIDWEST, KILLING 9. SOLAR-POWERED CARS TO BE ON HIGHWAYS BY YEAR-END. None of them said anything about a hot, sexy killer robot on the loose.

"Hey, isn't that where the ball falls on New Year's Eve?" Dover craned his neck to see the building's top.

"It is," Kate said. "Oh my God!"

"What is it?" Gabe's heart leapt. Was Trina on the street? Maybe they could find her before she even got to the store. Gabe would just jump out of the car, and she'd run into his arms and—

"Look at the line outside Barnes & Noble!"

The others followed her gaze northward up Broadway. A huge line of people half a sidewalk deep snaked from the front of the bookstore, on the corner of Forty-third and Broadway, all the way down to Forty-second Street and around the corner.

"We're just going to have to badge security." Horton glanced at the clock on the dash. "Even if they start letting people in now, we don't have time to wait."

"It's worse than that," Kate said. "We don't have time to park."

It was true, Gabe saw, looking around him. There was no parking on Forty-second Street at all, and judging by the speed at which they were moving, they wouldn't have time to go around the block before Dr. Phil arrived.

"We're going to have to park on the sidewalk," Horton said.

Kate looked at Horton's face. "Okay! Everyone hang on for a little off-roading!"

Gabe gripped the seat back as the SUV bumped effortlessly over the curb, sending pedestrians scattering and people in the line shrinking back against the wall. Dover bounced excitedly next to him. Gabe had to admit, it was pretty cool to watch shocked tourists try to get out of their way.

Kate pulled up near the end of the line. It was filled with people clutching books and DVDs by Dr. Phil. Middle-aged housewives who reminded Gabe of his mom huddled together, giggling and squealing. Many fans wore T-shirts bearing Dr. Phil's image; one man even had a photo of him painted on the back of his denim jacket.

Horton reached up under the sun visor, yanked out an official-looking placard with the NSA's eagle emblem stamped on it, and tossed it onto the top of the dash console, where it would be visible through the windshield.

"All right!" he shouted. "Everyone to the front of the line!"

Gabe practically threw himself out of the car, followed by Dover. Kate and Horton ran ahead of them, and Gabe was vaguely aware of flashes going off as he ran. Tourists were taking pictures of them, assuming they were important or famous. *Wow!* Gabe thought as he rounded the corner onto Broadway. Was this what it felt like to save the world? Because he had to admit, it felt pretty good.

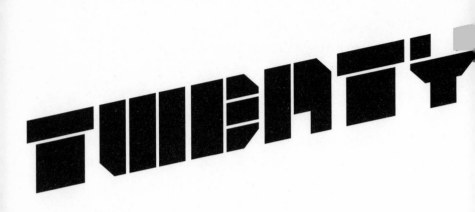

TWENTY

DELAY IS PREFERABLE TO ERROR.

—THOMAS JEFFERSON

THAT GOOD FEELING EVAPORATED AS GABE REACHED THE FRONT of the line, just behind Kate and Horton, and ahead of Dover.

A man wearing gray slacks, a navy blue blazer, and a badge that identified him as a member of Barnes & Noble's security team held up a forbidding hand to the group.

"I'm sorry," he said, politely but wearily, as though he'd had to repeat this speech many times over already, "but we're not allowing people into the store yet. You'll have to wait at the back of the line." He motioned toward Forty-second Street. "I know it looks bad, but everyone will get to come in. The line will start moving shortly."

Gabe looked around them. The store windows were plastered with posters announcing Dr. Phil's appearance, and others that showed Dr. Phil looking stern underneath assorted catchphrases such as GET REAL and HOW DOES THAT MAKE YOU FEEL? Gabe's eyes fell on lawn chairs, sleeping bags, pillows, and blankets. Thirty people at the front of the line had clearly slept there overnight, at the very least, to assure their spots. Farther back, curious passersby were asking people what they were waiting for. A couple of ragged-looking men cruised the line, rattling paper cups full of change, and a man with a booming voice was hawking copies of Dr. Phil's latest book.

"This is the only book he'll be signing today, people! Buy your copy now and you'll be guaranteed to meet the man himself!" Gabe watched as a middle-aged woman with frizzy orange hair, wearing a homemade T-shirt that read FAILURE IS NO ACCIDENT, waved the man over.

"I'm afraid we need to get inside immediately." Horton showed the guard his badge. "It's a matter of national security."

The guard was unmoved. "Sir, you are not the first person to approach me today asking to get into the store ahead of everyone else. I know you are anxious to see Dr. Phil speak, but as I said, everyone in line will have that chance. Now, if you don't mind . . ." He smiled and made a gentle shooing gesture with his hands.

Gabe could see that Horton was unused to receiving such treatment and wasn't about to handle it well. The older agent's face grew red and his mouth tight.

"Perhaps you don't understand," he said, allowing his jacket to fall open and reveal the holster that held his gun. "We have information that someone may attempt to assassinate Dr. Phil in your store."

"And I have information that you will be waiting in line." The smile dropped from the guard's face. "I've already spoken with seven women who claim to be pregnant with Dr. Phil's child, countless people who say they are related to him, and a man who swears God created him from one of Dr. Phil's ribs to be his life companion. There is nothing you can say to me that will compel me to let you through that door ahead of the people who have been here all night waiting for the exact same thing."

A couple of women near the front of the line wearing Snuggies and clutching teddy bears wearing Dr. Phil masks applauded. Horton was starting to attract attention now. Kate stepped in.

"We certainly don't want to cheat these people out of the opportunity to see their hero firsthand." She projected warmth and graciousness as she held up her badge. "In fact, we want to ensure that they get to meet him: We're here to save Dr. Phil's life," she entreated.

"Dr. Phil saves lives! He doesn't need some sorority chick wearing her dad's suit and her mom's shoes to save *his* life!" an alarmingly muscular old man just behind the lawn-chair brigade shouted.

Murmurs of "That's right!" and "You tell her how it *is*!" greeted his comment. Kate blushed. Horton exploded.

"Dammit," he shouted, "we are representatives of the National Security Agency, affiliated with the United States government, and we're here to prevent the assassination of a widely known television personality! I *demand* that you let us in!"

"I will let you in, sir, when it is your *turn*." The guard was still managing to maintain an outward demeanor of calm, but veins were beginning to throb in the man's beefy neck.

Horton moved right up in the guard's face. "I will not be stopped by some Saturday-afternoon rent-a-cop who doesn't know the law!" he screamed, spittle flying.

"Actually, sir," the guard took a step back and reached for the Motorola walkie-talkie on his belt, "I work as a 'rent-a-cop' here"—Gabe could practically see the air quotes around the phrase—"to pay for my education at the John Jay College of Law. And *that's* where I learned that the NSA was created during the Truman administration to handle cryptologic intelligence. That means to handle the coding and decoding of information," he added condescendingly. "Excuse me a moment, please." He brought the Motorola to his mouth.

"Code D at the front, I repeat, we have a Code D at the front," he barked into the walkie-talkie.

"Do you think I don't know when the agency I've given my *life* to was created, or what it does?" Horton raged.

"I don't know anything about you, sir." The guard coolly replaced the device at his belt. "But I *do* know that the NSA is not involved in field ops and that, by law, they are limited to the gathering of foreign intelligence. So I can't think of a single reason you might be here except that you are in severe need of advice from Dr. Phil. And *that*," he concluded, indicating the line, "doesn't make you special."

A cheer rose from the assembled throng, and Horton lunged at the guard. At that moment four other large men wearing the blue blazers of the Barnes & Noble security team burst out of the bookstore's doors and surrounded him and Kate. The largest of them laid a restraining hand on Horton's shoulder.

"I'll have to ask you to come with us, sir," he said. "You too, ma'am." He nodded at Kate.

The large guard unhooked a pair of handcuffs from around his belt and yanked Horton's wrists behind his back. *Oh my God!* Gabe and Dover stared at each other. Kate and Horton were getting arrested! By bookstore cops! Was that even possible?

Horton realized what was happening and began to struggle violently. Kate attempted to step away from the group but was blocked by another guard.

"Cuffs or no cuffs," he said, holding a silver pair in front of her. "Your call. But you're going in either way."

Gabe looked over at Horton. Three guards, including the one who had originally been at the door, were holding the furiously writhing agent, while the big guard cuffed him.

"I'll have your jobs for this!" Horton shouted. "I'll have you all arrested for obstruction of justice, for assaulting an agent of the U.S. government, for—"

"Get real!" the old man who'd heckled Kate yelled. The crowd went wild. Flashes popped again and again, exploding in front of the giant neon flag on the side of the Times Square Armed Forces Recruiting Station. Gabe cast an uneasy eye toward the garish blue-and-red glow. Should he run over there and ask whoever was working for help? Or would they be on the side of bookstore security? He glanced back at Horton, who was shouting like a crazy man. Maybe it was best not to take any chances.

"Can you tell me where you're taking us?" Kate asked the guard who'd offered her the handcuffs, casting Gabe a meaningful glance. What was she trying to tell him?

"You'll both be taken to the store's holding cell until the proper authorities can be summoned," the man said.

Gabe gawked. *Holding cell*? He'd heard that Macy's, the big department store farther downtown, had one of those—but he'd always assumed it was a relic of the 1800s, or whenever the store had been founded. Barnes & Noble had their own *jail*?

He didn't have time to contemplate its existence further, because Kate—handcuff-free, he noticed—and Horton were being hustled into the store by the army of security guards as the crowd jeered and whistled. Just as the door was about to close behind them, a man wearing a flowered bedsheet and a gold unitard darted past Gabe and Dover and up to the entrance. The first security guard halted him just before he slipped in the door.

"I'm sorry, sir," the guard said, "but you'll have to wait in line like everybody else."

"But you don't understand!" the man babbled. "I'm a superhero sent from space to rescue Dr. Phil. If I don't get in there *right now*, off-worlders from Zamulon may attempt entry through the pages of the books."

"You'll have your chance to rescue the doctor in just a few minutes, when the line starts moving, sir," the guard said.

"They'll suck his brains out through his eyes!" the man howled.

"The line starts right around the corner," the guard said, pointing.

The man drew up his flowered sheet as though it were the wings of a bat, and then, pulling the fabric around himself Dracula-style, departed toward Forty-second Street. Gabe and Dover looked after him.

"Well," Dover said, "I guess that explains why they weren't so anxious to believe Kate and Horton."

"Yeah," Gabe agreed. "I have to admit, I'm a lot more freaked out by my mom's Dr. Phil addiction than I was before."

"Come on," Dover said. "She's nowhere near as crazy as that guy."

"True. But she's about two steps away from the Ladies of the Lawn Chairs." Gabe nodded at the all-nighters, who were chanting "How does that make you feel?" after the departing would-be superhero.

The guard turned and focused an eagle eye on Gabe and Dover. Gabe felt his heart plummet. Were they going to be thrown in Barnes & Noble jail, too? How were they going to find Trina and protect Dr. Phil?

"Can I help you gentlemen?" The guard asked.

That was when Gabe realized: The guard had no idea that he and Dover were with Kate and Horton!

"Uh . . . is it true that everyone waiting will really get in?" asked Gabe.

The guard nodded. "If you head for the back of the line now, you'll just make it: They're going to start letting people in in just five minutes."

"Thanks so much." Gabe and Dover took off down the line. Nobody was taking pictures this time. How fleeting was fame!

"Hey." He nudged Dover. "If we had this much trouble getting in—if *Kate* and Horton had this much trouble getting in—doesn't that mean Trina might have problems too? We should look for her in the line!"

"I dunno," Dover said. "Beautiful women usually have no problem getting where they want to go."

"With you," Gabe snorted. "But Kate and Horton had *NSA badges*, and they couldn't get in."

"And Kate's pretty beautiful herself," Dover said. "All right. You're on."

Slowly, they made their way down the line, scrutinizing faces. Gabe was amazed by how many different kinds of people had turned out to see Dr. Phil. He had thought they would all be middle-aged women, like his mom, but there were businessmen, teen girls, tattooed bike messengers, construction workers on break, thrash-metal boys in tight jeans and fat high-tops, and a gaggle of lady cops.

And then, of course, there were the fanatics, clutching home-made signs asking Dr. Phil to marry them or sporting homemade papier-mâché masks of the doctor's face. Didn't these people have anything better to do with their lives? Then he remembered going to a *Halo* convention with Dover when they were eleven, dressed as Captain Jacob Keyes and an Elite Ranger, respectively. Suddenly he felt much less judgmental.

They rounded Forty-second Street without having seen any sign of Trina. The line stretched well past the SUV, which was still pulled up on the sidewalk.

"Ugh," he said. "This is hopeless."

"The guard said everyone would get in," Dover reminded him, as they passed the SUV, which, Gabe noted with remote pleasure, still didn't have a parking ticket on it. At least the NSA badge worked *somewhere*!

"If Trina's already in there, we don't stand a chance of saving Dr. Phil before she gets to him." What if she were armed? What if *that* was what she'd been doing all day? Gun shopping? Or would she just use her bare hands, like Horton had said? Would she be happy to see Gabe . . . or would she kill him to get to Dr. Phil?

"We do if they don't bring him out before everyone gets inside," Dover pointed out. "Besides, we still have half a block to go, so we still have a shot at finding her."

"Maybe not!" Gabe shouted, as a cheer rose from the throng. "The line is moving!"

TWENTY ONE

LOVE IS A MANY-SPLENDORED THING.
—FRANCIS THOMPSON

THE LINE WAS INDEED MOVING—A WHOLE FIVE FEET.

"I guess they can't let everyone in at once or it would be mayhem, but *come on*!" Gabe hopped from foot to foot.

"THE ONLY BOOK HE'LL BE SIGNING!" a voice howled in his ear. It was the man who had been selling books at the front of the line. He held out a copy of the new book that Dr. Phil would be signing. "TWENTY-FIVE DOLLARS!" Gabe looked down at the book. It was called *Free Advice*. He snorted.

"Thanks, but I'll pass."

"IT'S THE VALUE OF A LIFETIME! TWENTY-FIVE DOL-LARS GUARANTEES YOU TWO POINT FIVE SECONDS WITH THE GREAT MAN HIMSELF!"

"That's a good point," Dover reasoned.

"Ten dollars a second is good? Query: Have you lost your mind?"

"No, I haven't," Dover said. "But think about it—we need the opportunity to get as close to him as possible. Especially if we can't manage to find her beforehand."

"All right." Gabe extracted two crumpled tens from his pocket.

"Plus, we've got to have *something* to show for waiting in this line," Dover said.

"I don't have any more money." Gabe turned out his pockets. "Do you have a five?" Dover shook his head.

"No problem," the salsesman yanked the tens out of Gabe's hand before he could pocket them again. "Special sale!" He thrust a copy of *Free Advice* into Gabe's hands and moved off.

"Hey!" an irate man a few people ahead of Gabe and Dover shouted, waving his copy of the book angrily. "I paid twenty-five! I want my money back!"

"Look inside and see if the pages are blank," Dover said. "You know, like when you buy a DVD player off the street and there's just a brick inside the box."

"I think that would be a pretty dangerous game with this crowd," Gabe said, cracking the book nonetheless. "Nope, it's filled with advice. *'Quit crying and get back in the saddle that burned you.'* What?"

"I'm kind of starting to see where your dad is coming from," Dover commented. "Hey, we're moving again!"

After ten minutes that seemed like hours, they had almost reached the front door. Eager fans had torn some of the posters away as they entered the store. The guard who had tangled with Horton and Kate was still there, waving people through. Gabe suddenly had an awful thought.

"It's going to be a lot harder to stop Trina with just the two of us—and no weapons." He turned to Dover.

"'*No one can out-you you,*'" Dover read. "'*Carry on: You are there.*'"

"Will you shut that?" Gabe yelled. "We're approaching D-Day here, and we've got nothing!"

"We don't have nothing." Dover closed the book. "Okay, we have next to nothing. Better call up those LARPing skills. Maybe you can make a shuriken out of a couple of CD cases."

"Be serious!" Gabe pleaded. "We're almost there!"

"Sorry. I think all that self-help talk went to my head."

"We need some kind of plan."

"I think we're going to have to rely on the same thing we were counting on at the UN," Dover said, "which is Trina recognizing you. After that, I guess we can just tackle her or something. Yeah," he looked excited. "I could tackle her!"

Gabe frowned. She might be a killer, but he didn't like that idea at all. He had another thought. "What if her main drive—to kill Dr. Phil—overrides the constants we reprogrammed? If she's in attack mode, she might not even recognize us!"

"Calm down," Dover said. "If she doesn't recognize us, we might have an even better shot at stopping her: At least she won't think to run from us."

The door opened again, and the beefy security guard who had cuffed Horton beckoned them in. Gabe thought briefly of asking him about Horton and Kate, but he didn't want to take any chances. They were on their own now. He stepped inside the store with Dover close behind him.

The scene was one of complete chaos. At the far end of the store was a podium with a microphone. Behind it hung a banner reading FREE ADVICE. In front of it sat an acre of chairs, already filled with chattering fans. People swarmed everywhere, yanking books and CDs from shelves, asking where the bathroom was, jostling to find a good spot from which to see their hero. On either side, escalators led to the second floor, which was open in the center, forming an atrium above the seating area. Zealous fans were already partially lining the Plexiglas balcony, shouting down to their friends about who could see better.

"Hey, look," Dover said, as Gabe became aware of the sound of cash registers ringing furiously. "You can buy the new book right here, too!"

Gabe looked in the direction Dover was pointing. There was a huge display of books, with a sign on top announcing SALE $16.99! "Dammit! That guy swindled us!"

"But not as badly as he swindled everyone else. As Dr. Phil would say—"

"Save it." Gabe put a hand up. "That way, I'll feel like I got my three extra dollars' worth."

"Are you planning on getting that signed?" a youngish woman standing nearby wearing a Barnes & Noble security uniform asked Dover, pointing to the book he was carrying.

"Um, uh . . . yeah!" he said. "Yeah, I am!"

The woman pointed to the far right wall of the store, where

an unruly line had formed. "That's the line to get books signed. Dr. Phil won't be signing until he's finished speaking, but if you wait there now, you'll have a head start on everyone else—well, *almost* everyone else." She smiled at Dover.

"How about if I hang out here with you?" Dover looked the woman up and down appreciatively. "What kind of head start will *that* give me?"

"Excuse me, my friend really needs to go use the bathroom right now. It's in this direction, right?" Gabe asked. The woman nodded. He grabbed Dover by the arm and yanked him away.

"Hey!" Dover said. "Why'd you do that? I was making *out!*"

"You were making an ass out of yourself. Besides, we need to focus on finding Trina. This place is crazy!"

"I was just being polite!" Dover protested. "And besides, I think it would be a good idea if we stood in line. At least from there, we can see pretty much the whole crowd."

"You're right." Gabe scanned the area. If he stood in back, he'd definitely be able to see over the heads of the seated audience members. But if anything happened—if Trina really showed—he wouldn't be able to get through the densely packed chairs. "Except I think just *you* should stand in line."

"What? You're gonna leave me all alone with the craziest people in here? Look, I'm sorry you paid too much for the book, but—"

Gabe interrupted him. "I'm gonna stand in the balcony; that way, we'll have both floors covered."

"That's a good idea," Dover admitted. "But what if one of us sees her? What do we do then?"

"You get your wish. Tackle her. There's no way you'll be able to get upstairs fast enough or I'll be able to get downstairs fast enough, so if she's on your floor, go for her."

"*Yes!*" Dover made a pumping motion with his fist. "On it! Hey, lay-deeez!" he shouted, making for the line. Several granny-aged women at the back of it giggled appreciatively and made room for him.

His heart pounding, Gabe made for the "up" escalator. He took its stairs two at a time, passing irate fans without a glance. Now that he and Dover were separated and had established their plan, he was fully focused on his mission.

At the top of the escalator, he hesitated briefly, searching for the best vantage point. He chose a spot just to the left of the balcony's center: From there, he would be able to see pretty much the entire floor. He'd also be nearest the "down" escalator, in case Trina was on Dover's floor, and he could monitor arrivals on the "up" escalator.

He surveyed the crowd closely as he approached his chosen spot. The area directly behind and to the left of him would constitute his only blind spot. He wanted to make sure Trina wasn't there before he turned his back on the space.

Trina. It was hard for him to get as worked up about seeing her as he had been at the United Nations. He had felt so let down upon not finding her there—or in any of the other eighteen locations they'd visited earlier in the day—that he was having trouble mustering excitement at the thought of catching her here. Sure, his dad hated Dr. Phil with a passion that bordered on the unholy—but had he *really* programmed her to kill him? And even if he had, who was to say that she didn't have a wire crossed somewhere and was just off running loose and losing power somewhere in the city? After all, she didn't appear to have assimilated any of the information Gabe had programmed her to respond to. She had come to New York City without visiting a single comic book store!

If they didn't find her here—or anywhere—he and Dover would have to return home without her, and Gabe would have to explain what had happened to his dad. And Milton would *never* forgive him. Would he disown him? Gabe felt as though he would almost rather face a gun-toting Trina than his father's wrath.

He was jerked from his thoughts by the high whine of feedback. A feverish-looking woman in a flowing skirt, ruffly shirt, and long ropes of pearls was at the podium, adjusting the microphone. Gabe was glad he couldn't smell her: She looked like she bathed in perfume. Giving one last searching look behind him, he took his spot at the balcony railing. Below him, Dover had somehow advanced farther up the line and was working on charming a mother and young twin daughters who were just ahead of him. He leaned a casual hand on the wall as he gestured in the air with the other—no doubt telling some stupid story, thought Gabe.

"Ladies and gentlemen," the woman spoke into the microphone with relish, "I know you've all waited a long time for this, so I won't make you wait any longer. Without further ado, I give you . . . Dr. Phil, with some free advice!" She giggled at her own joke and stepped away from the mic, but not before it transmitted the sound of her five-inch-long seashell earrings clacking against her neck.

Gabe gripped the railing. This was it. If Trina were here to kill Dr. Phil, he would have to see her now. Wouldn't he? Frantically, he scoured the balcony for a glimpse of her. People were still arriving at the top of the "up" escalator and running to jam themselves in among those already assembled at the balcony, but he didn't see Trina's flowered dress or her blonde hair anywhere.

On the floor, Dr. Phil walked toward the podium and waved at the crowd. Shrieks and screams greeted him. The tinny theme song of his show spilled from speakers anchored to the bottom of the balcony. People stood up out of their chairs and applauded and whistled as the doctor reached the lectern and simply stood there, basking in his fans' adoration.

And then Gabe saw her.

Her long, white-blonde tresses bouncing, she was just striding out from underneath the right-hand side of the balcony on long, tanned legs. She was still wearing the short, flowered summer dress she had picked out in the bedroom at the party. God, she was beautiful.

Gabe felt as though he'd been punched in the gut. All the feelings he'd been trying to repress came flooding back. He remembered his first sight of her under the glowing blue lights of the centrifuge at his father's house; the way she'd leaped on top of him in the gas station parking lot; the way she'd stuck up for him when Dover had thrown his phone out the window; the way she'd kissed him . . .

. . . *the fact that she was here to kill Dr. Phil.*

Gabe tore his eyes from Trina for a split second. She was close enough to Dover that he had to see her—he just had to! But Dover was staring transfixed at Dr. Phil. *What the hell?*

Gabe looked at Trina again. She was unzipping a little clutch—where had she gotten it? She *had* spent the day at Victoria's Secret!—and out of it she pulled a sleek, deadly, black gun.

No one else had noticed yet. The audience continued to applaud; Dr. Phil made calming motions; and Dover continued to gaze stageward. There was no way he could get to Trina in time. Gabe looked over at the "down" escalator. Hopeless. She was going to do it! Trina was going to kill Dr. Phil! Unless . . .

Gabe looked at the floor. Directly below him was an unoccupied strip of space behind the rows of chairs, left clear so that store employees and security could pass through. From where Gabe stood up above, it was a twenty-foot drop. Trina had rescued him once. Would she save him again? Gabe watched as she dropped the purse to the floor. She raised the gun with both hands in a swift and steady motion, pointing it straight at Dr. Phil. And then . . .

. . . in one smooth move Gabe was atop the railing.

"TRINA!" he shouted. Then he closed his eyes and dove off the railing. A sick, falling sensation flooded his body. He couldn't hear anything—not the crowd shrieking, not Dr. Phil gasping into the microphone, not his heart thudding thick and fast—and then suddenly he heard the clank of cold metal hitting the floor, the swish of delicate fabric . . . and then he was looking up into Trina's warm brown eyes, her face curtained by her long blonde hair.

"You . . . you saved me!" he managed to get out. Now that he was in Trina's arms, he couldn't believe his plan had actually worked. She'd dropped her gun and abandoned her mission, all to save Gabe. "But . . . why?"

"Because"—the corners of her mouth lifted in a little smile—"you heart robots."

Gabe's features twisted in confusion. Suddenly, he remembered the photo of himself wearing an I HEART ROBOTS shirt from his Facebook profile. He *had* managed to download those profiles successfully after all! And Trina had known all along that he loved her.

And . . . maybe she loved him, too? After all, she had overridden her mission drive, overridden his own programming, to save his life. She had essentially sacrificed everything she was for him. If that wasn't human—if that wasn't love—then what was?

He gazed up at her. God, his heart hurt so bad! Her eyes seemed to grow bigger, her pillowy, pink lips to get closer— and then Gabe realized: She was leaning in to kiss him.

He reached around her slender back, drawing her close. As her lashes fluttered shut and her warm mouth met his, Gabe let his eyes close and his hand drift down her back . . .

. . . and he found the switch.

And he let her go.

TWENTY-TWO

WHERE IS HUMAN NATURE SO WEAK AS IN THE BOOKSTORE?

—HENRY WARD BEECHER

AS TRINA COLLAPSED ONTO HIM, GABE BECAME PAINFULLY AWARE of the silence. Not the isolated, distant silence his brain's sky-rocketing endorphins had cast him into as he fell, but real, honest-to-God, pin-drop silence.

He also became aware of Trina's breasts, which were now pressing into his chest as he lay prone on his back. *Uh-oh.* He shifted her slightly in an attempt to stem the rising tide of physical attraction that threatened to flood his body. As her flaxen hair slid away from his face, he realized that several hundred Dr. Phil fans were staring at him in shock and horror—as was Dr. Phil himself, frozen at the podium.

Oh, no! Gabe realized what the scene must look like to the assembled throngs. IS THERE A DOCTOR IN THE HOUSE? the headlines would scream. DERANGED FANBOY LEAPS FROM BALCONY AT DR. PHIL FORUM, IS RESCUED BY STUNNING BLONDE, KILLS HER! He froze. Should he struggle to get her off him? Should he act as though she had passed out? Should he start kissing her passionately? Maybe people would think they were a couple given to extreme forms of PDA . . .

"Oh my God!" a woman shrieked. "He's got a *gun!*"

The gun. Gabe had totally forgotten about it. He turned his head and saw the deadly looking black weapon lying several feet away. Most people in the crowd couldn't see that no one was holding it, however, and the woman's words triggered a stampede. People ran for the walls, the escalators, the exits—anywhere they could get that was far away from Gabe, the assassin. They dropped their copies of *Free Advice* and knocked over chairs as they went. Gabe tried to roll on top of Trina to shield her from the kicking, trampling feet—What if she were damaged? What if someone accidentally turned her back on?—but he was prevented by the throngs shuffling around him. A stentorian shout halted his efforts.

"EVERYBODY FREEZE!"

Oh God. Was he going to be arrested? How could he possibly explain himself?

It was the security guard who had read Horton the riot act earlier—only now he was *with* Horton . . . and Kate!

"Give them room!" the guard shouted as Horton and Kate rushed toward the still-prostrate Gabe. Kate knelt beside him as Horton gingerly rolled Trina off him.

"Wh-where are your handcuffs?" Gabe stuttered. "How did you get out of B&N jail?" He struggled to sit up.

"We explained everything to the security guard—"

"Not everything," Horton snapped.

"Well, we didn't tell him Trina is a robot, but we finally managed to convince him that someone was going to attempt to assassinate Dr. Phil here today. We got out just in time to see you jump. If it hadn't been for you, Dr. Phil would be dead." Kate looked at him warmly, and Gabe felt his cheeks heating up. He was a hero! But at what cost? He had betrayed Trina, the girl—the robot—he loved.

Horton had gently laid Trina down to his left and lifted her arms up off the floor, placing them across her body. Now he unhooked a pair of handcuffs from his belt.

"Hey! Why are you handcuffing her?" Gabe lowered his voice. "I turned her off! You don't need those!"

"To the contrary," Horton hissed. "We *do* need these. If she were a human assassin, we'd bring her out cuffed. We don't need to raise our profile any more than we already have."

Gabe could see his point, but he still winced as Horton clamped the icy steel bracelets around Trina's delicate wrists. He knew she couldn't feel the cuffs, but still . . .

"All right." Horton picked up the gun and stood. "You're going to be the one to carry her out of here," he said to Gabe. "I'll clear a path, and Kate will bring up the rear. We're going to go straight out the front and to the car. Do you copy?"

Kate placed a solicitous hand on his arm. "Are you up to this?"

Gabe nodded. Where was Dover? Looking around, he didn't see his alleged best friend anywhere. Hadn't he seen him throw himself off the balcony? Gabe could have been killed while Dover was getting some grandma's Jitterbug digits. Dover hadn't even known Trina was in the store until Gabe took a potential death dive into her arms!

"I'm okay," he said to Kate.

Together, they rose from the hard, wooden floor. Gabe leaned down and scooped Trina into his arms. She was still warm, and her cuffed hands rested in her lap, making her look more vulnerable than ever. Gabe wished he could just run with her, run down the street, away from Kate, from Horton, Dover—everyone, and just have everything always be as it had been that night at the party when they were kissing.

But that wasn't how it would be, he reminded himself. Trina was a killer—if he were to switch her on right now, she'd try to get away and kill Dr. Phil again. Exhaling, he pulled her close against him. If this was his last chance to hold her, he was going to make the most of it.

Ahead of him, Horton briskly made his way through the uneasy crowd. Though the Dr. Phil fanatics had stampeded at the first sign of danger, most of them had only gotten as far as the front of the store before Kate had arrived on the scene and neutralized the situation. Now they milled about, reluctant to leave the presence of their hero. Gabe followed behind Horton, trying his best to ignore the curious stares that followed him and Trina as they made their way out of the store. He saw several camera phones filming and put his head down. He didn't know where the footage was going to wind up, but he certainly didn't need his dad to find out about Trina's daring escape—and his part in it—on the evening news.

"She should get the death penalty!" one woman yelled as he passed.

"Is this going to be on TV?" a man yelled—Gabe thought it might be the old guy who had been rude to Kate outside the store.

"TV? Dude, it's already viral on 4chan!" said a long-haired boy wearing a shredded T-shirt and a necklace that looked like it was made out of metal thorns.

"Hey, she looks heavy. Lemme hold her for ya, buddy," a fortyish man in a sweatsuit leered, leaning forward and putting out his hands as though to touch Trina or take her away from Gabe.

Gabe jerked her away and heard Kate admonishing the man behind him. These people were *crazy*! He had to get Trina out of here! Ahead of him he saw the door open, and he felt cool air rush in—he was almost at the exit!

Then there was a whooshing sound and someone slammed into him from behind, putting an arm around his neck in a wrestling chokehold. Gabe's eyes widened in terror. Who—?

"Hey, man, trying to make your getaway without me?"

Dover.

Gabe shook his arm off and hurried out the door. "Where have you *been*?"

Dover kept pace alongside him as they headed down Broadway at a rapid clip. At least they weren't drawing nearly as many stares here. But mostly he was just mad. He tried not to let it show, staring straight ahead.

"I got your book signed!" Dover held up the copy of *Free Advice* Gabe had bought while waiting in line. "Here, look!"

Gabe ignored him. Dover reached around so that the book was practically in his face. Gabe nearly broke stride, but the sight of Horton hotfooting it down the street ahead of him reminded him to keep pace. "Unbelievable," he muttered.

"Yeah, it pretty much is. I guess he was so stoked to be alive that he just started signing stuff for everyone who was waiting in the line instead of making them wait until after. Not like they're not all going to stick around to hear him speak," Dover added. "Those people are nuts!"

Gabe wished Dover would stop talking. What kind of friend was he? Gabe had risked his life by *throwing himself off a balcony onto a gun-wielding robot*, and Dover had been getting a book—which he, Gabe, had paid for—signed. Hot tears welled up in his eyes and threatened to spill over. His life was in ruins. The only girl he had ever loved—and who had *loved him back*—was gone. His father was either going to kill him or ground him for life, and his lifelong best friend was turning out to be a grade-A jerk. One of the tears made its way past his lashes and coursed down his cheek.

"Hey, hey!" Dover said, sounding concerned. "Why the tears? You're a *hero*! You're already eight kinds of famous on the Internet. You're in New York City, walking through Times

Square with a stone-cold fox you know how to turn on lying helpless in your arms! I mean, what else could you want out of life?" he finished exasperatedly as they turned the corner onto Forty-second Street. "Why are you being such a . . . a *pussy*?"

Gabe halted. That was it. He couldn't take anymore.

"Why am I being such a *pussy*?" he yelled. "Why are you being such a *dick*?" He was dimly aware of Kate drawing closer to them from behind, but he couldn't stop now.

"You've been a jerk ever since we found Trina—no, ever since my parents left!" he shouted.

Dover looked astonished. "What—what are you talking about?"

"First you wouldn't leave me alone until we broke into the lab; then you wanted to have sex with Trina; *then* you threw my phone out the window of a moving car; and *now* you come to me after I threw myself off a frigging balcony because you were too busy gawking at Dr. Phil to remember where the hell you were, and you call *me* a pussy?" he raged. "Where the hell were you when I was taking my life in my hands to save a guy you were bitching about not ten minutes earlier?"

Dover's expression morphed from one of astonishment to outrage. "Oh, *I'm* a dick?" He thumped his chest. "*I'm* a dick? Who hogged Trina from the moment we saw her? Who laughed at my corduroys when the school bully was making fun of them? Who—"

"Let's GO!" Horton shouted up ahead. He had reached the SUV and unlocked it and was gesturing frantically to the boys from the open back door.

"Come on!" Kate said breathlessly as she brushed past them. She caught the keys Horton tossed to her and went around to the driver's seat.

Gabe gave Dover an angry glare and started for the SUV. Horton was waiting in the back and reached out to take Trina from him.

"I've got her," Gabe said shortly. A strange expression flitted across Horton's chiseled features, but he drew back, and Gabe climbed in. Carefully, he laid Trina down on the floor. He hadn't noticed it when they found her, but now he couldn't get over how strange it was not to see her breathing. Or "breathing," he thought sorrowfully as he straightened up, still looking at her. Had Trina ever really been alive—or had Gabe just wanted to believe that?

Dover threw himself into the front seat and slammed the door. He tossed the book into the back, and it landed near Gabe. He angrily kicked it away. Kate started the engine, and with a roar and a bump, they were off the curb and speeding westward.

"Where are we going?" Dover fastened his seatbelt.

"NSA main headquarters in Fort Meade, Maryland." Kate turned down Ninth Avenue. "About four hours away."

"What's going to happen to Trina?" Gabe and Dover asked at the same time. Gabe frowned.

"The team at NSA will open her up and see what modifications your father made—apart from programming her to kill a TV shrink," Horton said dryly. "After they've reprogrammed her and updated her software, she'll most likely be deployed in the field as originally intended."

"The field?" So Trina wouldn't be gone forever after all! His head spun with visions of himself and Trina running through a grassy pasture, laughing, before collapsing among the wildflowers and making out passionately.

"Kyrgyzstan, the Ukraine, Afghanistan, Serbia—wherever the agency determines she's needed." Horton shifted away from the window and toward Gabe as the car entered the Lincoln Tunnel.

"Will she have to work as a maid?" Gabe asked, remembering the way she'd been dressed when they found her. He cast a glance at Trina's motionless form on the floor. He didn't like to think of her cleaning rich people's houses or being pawed by lecherous old politicians.

"She'll function in whatever capacity is necessary for her to carry out her mission," Horton replied.

"I bet she'll wind up in a brothel!" Dover bounced in the front seat.

"Will you *stop*?" Gabe exploded. He reached past Horton and pounded Dover's headrest.

"*You* stop!" Dover twisted around. "It's not like I'm talking about your girlfriend, okay?"

"You don't *know* what you're talking about!" Gabe felt anger wash over him again. "All you care about is sex!"

Ahead of them, the tunnel exit loomed, a strip of bright blue sky visible through the arching gap.

"*Me*?" Dover said. "You were the one getting naked with her in the bedroom!"

"All you do is push me and push me," Gabe yelled, as the SUV rocketed out of the tunnel and into the late-afternoon sunlight, "and then when I actually do what you were pushing me to do, you get mad and jealous! You can't have it both ways!"

"What are you *talking* about?" Dover said. "I can't even make the connection here!"

He couldn't make the connection? He'd practically put Gabe's hands on Beverly's boobs the previous evening! Okay, not really, but he'd hounded Gabe about her rack, and how he should watch *Lord of the Rings* with her, and blah, blah, blah.

"You told me I should talk to girls," Gabe huffed, "and now you're all sore because I made out with Trina!"

"Okay." Dover leaned over his seat and counted on his fingers. "One, I told you you should talk to Beverly, specifically, because you were afraid to go over to her house, and two, you made out with a robot, not a girl!"

Gabe slapped Dover's hands and tumbled backward. *Oof.* "Do you notice how she's a robot when I make out with her, but she's a girl when *you* want to have sex with her?" he asked. "It's like you have this double—"

"Dick move," a female voice behind him said.

Trina? Gabe whirled around. Trina was groggily attempting to raise herself up from the floor. He must have bumped her power switch when he fell back! Terrified though he was, he couldn't help but admire her lithe beauty. God, she was—

"Oh, no, you don't." Horton placed a firm hand on her lower back. Instantly, she collapsed, her blonde hair spilling over her face. Gabe was glad. He didn't think he could stand to watch the life—or whatever it was—leave her eyes again.

"Pull over," Horton said to Kate. Immediately, she steered the SUV onto the shoulder of the turnpike, sending pebbles flying.

Gabe felt about six years old. Were he and Dover about to be reprimanded? What bullshit! He was going to get enough of this from his dad when he got back. He didn't need a lecture from Agent Horton, too.

"Turn off the ignition," Horton said.

Kate looked confused but did as he asked.

"Listen," Gabe said. "I'm sorry. We won't fight anymore."

"No, you won't," Horton said calmly. Then he reached into his jacket, pulled out his gun, and aimed it squarely at Gabe. "Get out of the car."

TWENTY THREE

I'VE GOT A BAD FEELING ABOUT THIS. —HAN SOLO

GABE'S BLOOD FROZE IN HIS VEINS AS HE STARED INTO THE BARREL of Horton's Glock Gen4. *Get out of the car?* There was nothing he wanted more than to get the hell out of the car! So what if they were on the shoulder of the New Jersey Turnpike? He'd walk home if he had to! Gabe's brain kicked into overdrive as he tried to process this turn of events. Was this some kind of tough-love thing? He had already apologized!

Kate was evidently thinking the same thing. "Roger!" she said in a shocked tone from the driver's seat. "What are you—?"

Horton whipped around to face her, training the Glock on her. "Give me your gun."

Gabe watched in horror as all the color drained from her face. "Oh my God," she whispered. "It's you."

"What's him?" Dover said in a high voice.

"Give me your gun!" Horton roared. But Kate was still frozen. The older agent placed the Glock's barrel against the side of Gabe's forehead. The metal was cool and heavy against his skin. Gabe felt the world begin to go white and realized he might faint.

"Give. Me. The. Gun," Horton said through gritted teeth. Kate fumbled awkwardly in her shoulder holster and handed over her pistol butt-first. Horton holstered it and, pulling his own gun a few inches back from Gabe's head, leaned across Gabe and threw open the car door. "Out."

Gabe moved clumsily toward the door and exited on the passenger side, away from the highway. His limbs were heavy, and he felt strangely distant from his body. His feet hit gravel with a crunching sound, and he had to steady himself on the car door for a moment. A semitrailer whooshed by just yards from the SUV, setting the vehicle rocking gently. Gabe looked behind him at oncoming traffic. Should he flag someone down? Would Horton shoot him? How was it possible that no one was seeing this happen? It was true no one could see the gun. He guessed cars broke down on the turnpike all the time. Or maybe it just looked like he had stopped to take a leak?

Inside the car, Horton said something unintelligible to Dover, who opened his door and stepped out as well. He looked as terrified as Gabe felt. Kate exited from the driver's-side door. It opened right onto the highway, and she looked so shaky that for a second Gabe was afraid she would stumble into traffic. But she pressed herself flat against the car and, reaching out, slammed the door shut. Then she sidled over to the front of the car and came down to where the boys were.

The entire time, Horton had kept his gun trained on Gabe but his eyes on Kate, as if he knew she were the only one who'd give him any serious trouble. Scared as he was, Gabe felt a brief surge of anger upon realizing this. Horton didn't consider him or Dover a threat. But maybe they could use that to their benefit.

As Kate rounded the front of the car, Horton exited through the door Gabe had come through, careful to keep his gun hidden behind his jacket.

"Turn around and walk." He made a jabbing gesture with the weapon.

Kate gave Gabe and Dover a helpless glance, and together the three started away from the highway, and into one of the vast fields stretching away from the turnpike. Horton followed closely. All around them, long grass waved. Occasionally, a blackbird flew up. Gabe stepped in what he thought was a puddle, but, looking down, he saw that the ground was wet and spongy in large patches. A large, juicy toad hopped across their path and disappeared.

These must be the New Jersey Meadowlands, Gabe realized. He had read all about the marshy area in ecology class, where they had studied the many different kinds of waterfowl that lived there. He remembered watching a DVD about dumping and other environmental abuses perpetrated on the ecosystem. Looking around, he saw huge factories in the distance, tangled metal structures that had the appearance of alien cities. One had multiple smokestacks, from which flames occasionally arose. The flames made him think of a crematorium. He shuddered. He didn't want to die out here!

"All right," called Horton. "Turn around!"

Slowly, Gabe turned. So did Kate and Dover. They were very far from the turnpike now: The roaring noise of traffic had become a faint hum, and the SUV looked lonely and small in the distance. Gabe wondered if the cops would find it and think it was broken down or abandoned. Would they look for its occupants out here? He didn't think so. Who would wander off this far into the marshes? Only someone who wanted to get lost, or die—or both.

Horton stood several yards away, smirking. Now that no one could see them, he had let his coat slip away from the gun, which he held casually at his side.

"I have to say," he said, looking up at the sky, "I never thought things would turn out this way." He brought his chin down and fixed Gabe with a level stare.

"Wh-what do you mean?" Gabe stammered.

"He means he's the one who's been planning to sell Trina to the North Koreans, and he didn't anticipate running into trouble," said Kate tightly from Gabe's right. Gabe looked over at her. She was still shaky, but she didn't look scared anymore—she looked angry. Gabe couldn't believe his ears. He looked back at Horton. The agent nodded.

"If someone offered you billions of dollars to steal a robot that cost millions to make," he said, speaking to Kate, "wouldn't you do it?"

Kate shook her head vigorously. "Hell, no, I wouldn't,

Roger!" she spat. "And I can't believe you would either. You've been an NSA agent for twenty-five years!"

"Exactly," Horton said calmly. "Twenty-five years I've served my country, and what am I going to have to show for it when I retire? Three gray suits, a head of gray hair, and a gray future of stretching my pension to make ends meet—and that's assuming the government actually *pays* my pension, instead of spending it on some killer blow-up doll," he sneered.

"Trina's not a doll!" Gabe shouted. Horton turned to him with an amused look on his face.

"Awwwwww," he cooed. "Somebody's getting protective of his robot girlfriend."

Gabe bristled, but Horton continued. "You know, your father wouldn't be stupid enough to fall in love with a robot. In fact, Milton is a very smart man—he was onto me months ago."

Kate gasped. "What?"

Horton nodded. "I received the offer from North Korea regarding Trina approximately one month before her completion. I don't know how—or even if—Milton got wind of it, but as soon as he was finished with her, he took her to his home lab. So in a way, you were right." He nodded at Gabe. "Your father *wasn't* building a super-secret killer robot in your house . . . but he *was* hiding her."

"From you?" Kate asked. "Milton knew? Then all that time we spent staking out the Messner residence . . ."

"... I was trying to find a time when Milton wouldn't be home, so I could steal Trina." Lifting the gun, he waved it at Gabe and Dover. "What I didn't count on," he said, "was two horny teenage geeks finding her, activating her, and then letting her get away."

Gabe felt dizzy. "You were watching our house? For how long?"

"For weeks."

"How did you find out that Gabe's parents were going away that weekend?" Dover asked. "There's no way you could figure that out just from watching the house—is there?"

"Bugs," Horton said simply.

"You bugged our *house*?" Gabe said. "You broke in? Why didn't you just take Trina then?"

"Kate and I were never in the house," Horton explained. "NSA tech ops ran the wires. As you know, your father is a very careful man. At first, we were monitoring him via the agency's intranet—that's basically the in-house web."

Gabe fought the urge to tell Horton that he knew what a frigging intranet was—he had reprogrammed the NSA's robot, for crying out loud!

"As I said, Kate and I work for internal affairs," Horton said. "I let the agency know I had received a tip that Milton might be preparing to sell Trina to a foreign power. They authorized the intranet monitoring, and that's how I learned about Trina's specifications—and how I was able to make the deal with North Korea."

"You used that information to sell Trina to the Koreans?" Kate managed. Her hair had come out of its ponytail on the trek through the marshlands and was loose and wild about her shoulders. She looked so very young and innocent. Gabe felt bad for her.

Horton nodded. "They were about to drop three billion dollars on her, and they wanted to know what they were getting. Can you blame them?"

Kate opened her mouth, but Horton went on. "At some point shortly after I began monitoring him at the agency offices, he made the decision to take Trina home. The agency wanted to bring him in then, but I knew that if they did, I'd never have a chance at Trina. It would be much easier for me to get her out of your house"—he nodded at Gabe—"than for me to sneak her out of the NSA's high-security labs. So I told the agency to let him go, and that I would monitor him. I specifically requested that Kate accompany me in order to deter any suspicion I might arouse if the case went on too long."

"Whoa," Dover broke in. "You pulled her in just to cover your ass? That's harsh." He shook his head.

Kate spoke, her voice hot with fury. "*That's* how I got my first field assignment? I can't believe this, Roger. I was so excited to be working with you—I looked up to you! Everyone told me how lucky I was to be working with you, how much I'd learn." She laughed bitterly. "I'm learning, all right."

Horton didn't seem to hear her. "I continued to monitor

Milton's actions through the intranet, trying to learn when I might have the chance to take Trina, but he only discussed the most technical details there. So I hacked into his personal e-mail to see what I could learn. But he has encrypted it so deeply, it can't be decoded using standard agency software."

Gabe felt a surge of pride. Of course his father had taken such extreme precautions that even a member of an agency centered on the gathering of foreign communications and cryptanalysis couldn't find his way in! He cast a glance at Dover, but Dover was transfixed by the gun in the gray-haired agent's hand.

"I didn't want to do a B and E—that's breaking and entering. I didn't want the agency to find out that I'd had access to the house when the time came to steal Trina. I needed to be completely above suspicion. Thanks to the bugs, we were able to ascertain that your parents would be gone this weekend.

"So," he finished, "that's how we came to be parked outside your house on Friday night. We were hoping to remove Trina from the premises after your parents left and you'd gone out for pizza or over to someone's house to play *Halo*." He smiled wryly. "We were a little concerned when you started looking for your parents' porn videos, thinking you might not leave the house if you found them, but thankfully, it turned out not to be an issue."

Gabe felt dirty. It was awful to hear Horton repeat back details of his and Dover's Friday night conversation *as if he'd been in the house with them*—which, in a way, Gabe realized, he had.

"I wish you'd stop using the term 'we,'" Kate snapped. "I felt bad enough about some of the tactics we used when I thought they were justified, but now"—she shivered—"I want no part of it."

"Kiddo, I never planned to cut you in on any part of it from the beginning." Horton brought the Glock up to his chest, cradling it. "I certainly didn't plan for things to end up this way, but now I have no choice." He leveled the gun at Gabe.

"Wait!" shouted Gabe. "You don't have to do this! You already have Trina in the car! Can't you just—can't you just leave us here?" *Where we can run back to the highway, flag down a car, borrow a cell, and have the state police stop your ass cold on the way to the airport?*

Evidently, Horton had already played out that same scenario.

"Sorry." He shook his head and cocked the trigger. Gabe closed his eyes. He was going to die. Or at least, his brain seemed to be telling him this. Gabe felt weirdly calm. This was it. The moment where his life was supposed to flash before his eyes. Would his father cry at his funeral? Would his father even come to his funeral? He wished he hadn't fought so much with Dover on this trip. He wished he could say good-bye to Trina.

"I promise to take good care of Trina," Horton sneered, as if reading his thoughts. "All the way to the airp—OW!!!"

Gabe's eyes flew open. Horton had dropped the gun and was dancing about, flailing his arms behind him. In a flash, Kate ran to the gun, picked it up, and trained it on Horton, who was too busy screaming in pain to notice. Kate began to snicker, and Horton, in his wild gyrations, turned to the side, giving Gabe a full view of the replica Legolas arrow that was lodged firmly in his right butt cheek.

Gabe stared. Legolas arrow?

Twenty yards ahead of him, a slender hand parted a clump of cattails, and out stepped . . .

"Beverly?" Gabe gasped.

"Hey, Gabe!" she called. "I hope you're planning on paying my parking ticket—and getting that broken window fixed!"

TWENTY-FOUR

IF YOU WANT A HAPPY ENDING, THAT DEPENDS, OF COURSE, ON WHERE YOU STOP YOUR STORY.
—ORSON WELLES

GABE COULDN'T BELIEVE HIS EYES. BEVERLY TSU HAD TRACKED them to the New Jersey Meadowlands and shot Horton with a replica Legolas arrow just as the renegade NSA agent had been about to kill Gabe and steal his father's robot? Warily he looked around. Then he pinched his thigh. He didn't appear to be dead, so . . . this must really be happening!

Beverly scampered across the field toward him, clutching her bow. A quiver of arrows—which Gabe recognized as being *LOTR*-regulation—rode on her back.

"Hi, Dover!" She halted before the two friends, offering her hand for a high five, which Dover delivered with gusto. "How's it going, Gabe?"

"Uh . . . it's going pretty good." Gabe took off his glasses and rubbed the bridge of his nose. "But I think I'm a little confused."

"Oh no!" Beverly put a solicitous hand on his arm. "Did you get pistol-whipped? I was on my stomach in the grass for a little bit there and couldn't see anything."

"No, I didn't get pistol-whipped," Gabe said as Dover moved off to stand next to Kate, who was guarding Horton with the Glock, making no effort to help him remove the arrow lodged in his butt.

"I'm confused because I have *no idea how you found us here*!" Gabe shouted. "Not that I'm not grateful you, uh, saved my life."

"I found you using LoJack," Beverly said. "My dad had it installed in the car when he got it for me; you know my parents don't have a lot of money, so he looked at it as protecting his investment, rather than as a frivolous expenditure."

Gabe found himself gazing at her glossy lips when she said the word *expenditure*. He realized that he would kind of like to see her say it again. Then he got ahold of himself.

"But Trina—the maid you saw run out of our house—parked it in Times Square early this morning," he said. "When did you get there? And how did you find us out here?"

"I took the train up and got there in the early afternoon. I saw the ticket on it and figured you'd be back. So I was waiting with the car when I saw you run out of the Barnes & Noble on Forty-third. I just followed you from there." She pointed to the highway. There, about thirty yards behind the SUV, Gabe could just make out the pale-green, domed top of the Beavle peeking out over the long grass.

"Wow," Gabe said admiringly, "you really do have Aragorn-level tracking skills, not to mention Legolas-level bow skills." Beverly looked down modestly.

"How did you know we were in danger?" he asked, pointing

to the bow. A faint wind began to ruffle the grass in an almost circular motion, and Gabe suddenly heard a faint mechanical noise begin and then grow nearer.

"Oh . . ." Beverly's long black hair whipped around her head, and the mechanical noise became louder, almost a roar. "Your dad told me you might be in danger."

"My *dad*?" Gabe's jaw fell open. Beverly smiled and nodded. She pointed to the sky.

"Yeah," she said. "You can ask him yoursel—"

Her last words were drowned out by the loud whupping sound of the rotor blades of a sleek black Bell Iroquois helicopter. It descended from above, landing a short distance behind them. A door on the side opened, and Milton Messner stepped out, followed by Gloria Messner and several NSA guards, all ducking to avoid the whirling blades as they ran. The Messners made a beeline for Gabe and Beverly, while the guards veered off toward Kate, Horton, and Dover.

Gabe's stomach churned as his father drew closer. He was wearing a loud, Hawaiian-patterned shirt Gabe had never seen. It screamed "vacation," but his lowered brows and downturned mouth screamed "rage." Gabe gulped. Did Milton know that Gabe had almost died protecting his creation? Maybe he knew and didn't care.

"Query!" Milton shouted over the throb of the helicopter blades. "What is the number-one rule?"

"Stay out of the lab," Gabe replied automatically, feeling

his stomach sink. Milton hadn't even been gone twenty-four hours, and in that span, Gabe felt like he'd lived a lifetime. And yet nothing had changed.

"I'm very upset with you, Gabe." Milton straightened up and looked disapprovingly at his son, his mouth a tight line. "Not only did you break the number-one rule, but you lied to me about it on the phone. And then you evaded me. Your mother was frantic." Gloria placed a hand on her husband's arm, but she was looking at Gabe. Her eyes brimmed with tears that threatened to spill onto her bright-pink tank top. Gabe couldn't help but notice that Milton had said that *Gloria* was frantic. No mention of how *he* felt about not being able to contact Gabe.

Milton continued. "I trusted you with our home and everything in it. I trusted you, and this is how you repay me: by placing my life's work at risk."

Gabe opened his mouth to apologize. A little beyond Milton's shoulder, his gaze landed on the NSA agents cuffing Horton. Two of them were holding him down while Kate clamped the metal bracelets around his wrists. Dover looked on, starry-eyed. Suddenly, Gabe realized . . . he wasn't sorry. Not at all.

"Oh yeah?" Gabe looked his father square in the eye. "Well, I trusted *you* my whole life, and how did you repay me? By lying."

Gloria gasped. "Gabe!" But Gabe pressed on.

"How come I never knew what you did for a living?" Gabe said. "I had to find out from a guy who was prepared to commit espionage using your robot. And another thing: I don't think it's cool that you work fourteen hours a day and ignore me and Mom. Don't get me wrong," he said, as Milton opened his mouth, "Trina is about the coolest gir—coolest piece of engineering on Earth, but maybe you could have taken a couple months more to make her and spent some of your face time with me and Mom."

Milton was red in the face. "Everything I've done, I've always done for you and your mother! I work for a highly secretive agency, and I've always tried to protect you from the perils connected with that. I certainly don't expect to be lambasted by my son for trying to keep the family safe!"

"Dad, when we first found Trina, I thought she was your mistress," Gabe said. "I thought that you had killed her and were hiding her in the basement." Gloria's face took on a stormy expression, and Mr. Messner looked taken aback.

"Gabe," he said, "Trina's . . . extreme appearance is a component of her intended function, just like her emotion-mirror programming or her internal GPS. I love your *mother*." He pulled Gloria close to him. "Not some robot!"

Gabe went on. "And then, later, when we were looking for Trina and trying to figure out what her mission was, Horton suggested you might have programmed her to kill the president—and I had to consider that you might have!"

"Y-you thought I would do something like that?" Mr. Messner said in a shocked tone.

"Only because you never tell me anything except what to do!" Gabe said. "I don't know who you are, and you don't know who I am!"

"Well," Milton admitted, "it's true that I've been less than forthcoming with you—and your mother." He looked down at Gloria and then back at Gabe. "But," he said gruffly, "I must have taught you *something*, since you were able to reprogram Trina."

Now it was Gabe's turn to be shocked. "You know about that?"

Milton nodded. "After the agency got ahold of me early this morning, they filled me in on what was going on."

"But how could they have known that I reprogrammed Trina?"

"Son, in an organization like this, everyone's watching everyone," Mr. Messner said, not unkindly. What he said next completely blew Gabe's mind. "I wish I could have been there to watch you reprogram her."

"Really?" Gabe's heart was beating fast.

Milton nodded. "I don't have to tell you how complex she is," he said with a meaningful look that caused Gabe to blush, "but all kidding aside, what you were able to do with her . . ." He shook his head. "Let's just say there are going to be some changes at the agency."

Gabe felt like he might burst with pride. His dad was

impressed with him! The NSA was reconsidering the design of its prize weapon because of him!

"It wasn't that hard," Gabe said modestly. "I mean, it was *really* hard to get in—to the lab and into Trina's mission drive," he said, excited to be talking about what he'd done with someone who truly understood—his dad! All those years of following in his dad's tech-geek footsteps, but from a distance. Never being able to *talk* about it. "Well, I didn't know it was her mission drive at the time, I mean, but—"

"I can't believe you kept your real job a secret from me, your wife, for *twenty years!*" Gabe's mom interrupted, fixing Milton with a death gaze. "What would Dr. Phil have to say about that? And you programmed a robot to *kill him*?" Poor Gloria was near tears. "You *know* he's my hero! And then you send my son on a dangerous mission—"

"Mom!" Gabe grabbed her by the shoulders. "He didn't send me—it was my choice! I wanted to go!"

"You—you wanted to protect Dr. Phil?" She asked hopefully.

"Yes! I mean no! I mean, I didn't know that's what Tri—I didn't know that's who the robot was programmed to kill." Gabe looked over at his father, who raised his eyebrows and tilted his head ever so slightly at Gabe.

"I mean, yes, definitely. I know how much Dr. Phil means to you. But Dad didn't really mean for her to kill Dr. Phil." He looked into his mother's wet eyes. "He meant it as a joke, okay?"

"I'd like to see this robot your father invented." Gloria blew her nose. Over her shoulder, Gabe could see his father shaking his head vigorously. "Did you say it was in the car?" she asked, peering toward the highway. "Maybe I could—"

She was mercifully interrupted by an NSA guard, who approached Gabe.

"Gabriel Messner?" Gabe nodded, feeling nervous. What now? "You have an urgent call, sir." The man handed Gabe a cell phone. "Also, we found this in the car. It belongs to you?" It was a copy of Dr. Phil's book *Free Advice*. Gabe nodded. The guard handed him the book and moved off to stand at a respectful distance.

Gabe looked around. Dover was still with Kate; his parents were right next to him. Who could be calling?

"Hello?"

"Gabriel Messner? Phil McGraw here." Gabe nearly dropped the phone.

"Um, hey, Dr. Phil." Gabe looked at his mom, whose eyes went wide. "How's it going?" Gabe asked.

"Never better," the shrink boomed. "I'm just calling to thank you for saving my life this afternoon."

"Oh, it was my pleasure," Gabe said.

"Well . . ." Dr. Phil chuckled. "It looked like it might have been a bit of a pleasure at that, hey?" Gabe blushed. "But seriously," Dr. Phil said, "I am most grateful, and if there's any way I can ever repay the favor, I hope you'll let me know."

Gabe smiled. "Actually," he said, motioning to Gloria, "there *is* a way you can repay me." He handed the phone to his mother. "Dr. Phil wants to talk to you."

Gloria took the device in trembling hands and held it up to her ear. "H-hello?" Gabe could hear a faint crackling sound as Dr. Phil introduced himself. Gloria Messner squealed. "It *is* you!" she shouted. "Oh, Dr. Phil, I've watched your show every day since . . ." Her voice grew faint as she wandered off clutching the phone. Gabe's glance met his father's, and they shared an eye roll. Enough Dr. Phil already!

Gabe looked down at the book in his hand and frowned. It didn't matter that he'd saved Dr. Phil's life or that his mom was on the phone with the celebrity shrink right now. When Gabe looked at *Free Advice*, all he saw was the twenty dollars he'd spent to buy it. And Dover had gotten it signed, so he probably ought to give it to him anyway. Sighing, he flipped to the title page to see Dr. Phil's autograph. He froze with his hand in midair when he saw the inscription:

TO GLORIA MESSNER, FROM HER BIGGEST FAN. —DR. PHIL

Just then, he felt a hand on his shoulder.

"Hey!" Dover said, looking down. "Did you get to show it to your mom yet?"

"No. She's . . . on the phone." Gabe looked up at his friend. "You got this signed for my mom?"

"Yeah." Dover shrugged. "I mean, she's his biggest fan.

You'd already taken care of business with Trina and all, so I figured I'd do my part. Do you think she'll like it?"

"Like it? Dude, she's going to *love* it."

"Listen." Dover rubbed the back of his neck. "I want to apologize for being a jerk. You were right—I was being really pushy, about breaking into the lab, turning Trina on . . . *every-thing*. And I'm sorry I threw your BlackBerry out the window." He blew out a long sigh. "It's just . . . I guess I just wanted us to have an adventure, you know? I didn't realize it would get quite this out of hand, though!"

Gabe looked at the book. Even when they had been mad at each other and fighting, Dover had been thinking of him. Deep down, he knew Dover hadn't meant to hurt him. He had always been Gabe's best friend—and he still was.

Gabe shook his head. "Don't be sorry," he said. "I know I can be a stick-in-the-mud sometimes, and you were just trying to help me." He coughed. "I mean, it's true we could have died . . ."

"We could have gotten Dr. Phil killed, too," Dover pointed out.

"Yeah." Gabe watched his mom wander through the weeds, gabbing with her hero. "But you know what? It was the most fun I ever had."

"Me too."

"Hey!" Gabe said, remembering. "What happened with Kate? You were hitting on her pretty hard earlier. Did you give up?"

Dover snorted. "She told me to come find her in about ten years."

The two friends laughed, then were silent for a moment.

"Hey, Gabe?"

"Yeah?"

"You wanna see if we can run to the car and say good-bye to Trina?"

A wide grin spread slowly over Gabe's face, and he held up his hand for a high five.

"Dove," he said, "COUNT ME IN!"

Gabe and Dover took off running through the tall grass. When they arrived at the SUV, three navy-clad NSA guards were already there.

"I'm afraid I can't let you boys in," the oldest guard, a Japanese man with shockingly taut musculature and kind eyes, said. In his hands he cradled an Armalite AR-18. The other two guards were similarly equipped.

Gabe gulped. Maybe this wasn't such a good idea after all. He looked at the SUV's tinted rear windows. He couldn't see Trina, but he knew she was in there. He couldn't just walk away.

"Please," he begged the guard. "I promise I won't take a minute. I'll leave the door open."

"I'm sorry," the man said sympathetically. "But you'd have to have top-level clearance to get inside that car. I don't even have permission to open the door myself. I—"

The Qualcomm at his ear glowed, and he reached up to touch it.

"Yes?" It was clear he was no longer speaking to Gabe. He straightened up. "Sir! Yes, sir! Absolutely! Thank you, sir!" He nodded into the distance.

Gabe turned around. Far away in the field, his father waved and turned away.

"Agent Messner has given you clearance to enter." The guard was awestruck. He reached out to shake Gabe's hand. "You must be a pretty big deal, son."

Gabe's heart swelled with pride as he shook the man's hand. After everything that happened, his father trusted him with Trina.

"I'll wait out here," Dover told Gabe. "Hey!" he said to the guard. "Have you ever gotten to fire that thing?" He pointed to the gun. "Is it as badass as it looks? Are chicks impressed by it?"

Gabe shook his head and moved toward the SUV. Opening the rear door, he crawled inside. Trina lay on her side on the scratchy gray and black carpet where she'd fallen earlier. Carefully, Gabe reached around and pressed the small of her back. He brushed her hair back from her eyes. He wanted to see animation come back into them for the last time. He watched the tiny power bar load, and then . . .

"Hey." Warmth flooded her eyes as she spoke. "What's happening?" She reached up to touch his cheek. "You look sad."

Gabe's throat felt tight, and tears welled at the corner of his eyes. He fought them back. "I just . . . I just came to say good-bye," he said. "I don't know where you're headed, or what your next mission will be, but I wanted to tell you . . ." He heaved a deep breath. "That I'll miss you."

Trina dropped her hand from his cheek and pushed herself up into a sitting position. She put her hands on his shoulders and leaned her forehead against his. He stared deep into her beautiful brown eyes. It just didn't seem possible that she wasn't human.

"I'll miss you, too," she said. "But even if we didn't have to say good-bye, we couldn't be together anyway. You deserve a real girl." She nodded over his shoulder.

Gabe turned his head. In the distance, Beverly was talking to his father. Her long black hair blew about her bare shoulders in the breeze. She was laughing. He turned back to Trina. She raised her eyebrows. He swallowed hard but nodded. He knew she was right.

"Besides . . ." She smirked. "I was able to override my mission drive this time, but who knows? Next time I might just let you drop twenty feet."

"Thanks a lot." Gabe grinned. "But I don't see how that makes you all that different from a real girl." They both laughed.

"Gabe!" A shout sounded from outside the car. Gabe and Trina looked out the window. Dover was waving his arms.

"We gotta jet, dude! Chopper's leaving!" The grass behind him began to stir as the Bell's rotor warmed up.

Gabe turned to Trina. "I have to power you down before I go," he said. "I hate to do it."

"Then don't." Taking one of her hands from his, Trina reached behind her back. Gabe stopped her.

"If I ever get to stop by the lab," he said, taking her other hand in his and holding it tightly, "I promise I'll come by and visit."

"Do that," she said, smiling. She leaned up and kissed him softly on the cheek. "Maybe I'll remember you." She grinned. Then her hand went limp in his and she slumped in his arms, her eyes fluttering closed.

Gabe stared at her for a long moment, taking in her rosy lips, her delicate eyebrows, her velvety lashes for the last time. Then he laid her carefully on the floor of the car. Her white-blonde hair spread out like a halo around her head. The burning orange light of the setting sun lit her beautiful face, and dusky shadows danced across her flowered dress. Gabe hesitated.

"GABE!" It was Milton's voice this time.

"Coming!" Gabe yelled.

He rose halfway to his feet, then stopped. Gently, he leaned down and kissed Trina's perfect, still-warm cheek. "You might not remember me," he whispered, "but I'll always remember you."

Then he stood up and went to join his father. He was waiting for him.

EPILOGUE

THERE'S A GIRL RIGHT NEXT TO YOU, AND SHE'S
JUST WAITING FOR SOMETHING TO DO.

—STEPHEN STILLS

"DO YOU WANT BUTTER ON YOUR POPCORN?" BEVERLY CALLED AS she walked to the kitchen. It was Saturday night, just a few weeks later, and Gabe was delivering on his promise of watching the entire *Lord of the Rings* trilogy with her at one sitting. Though the original agreement had been that all the lights would be off, it had proved too dark for snacking, so they had settled for leaving on a single string of white Christmas lights, which glowed warmly from the Alberta spruce tree Mr. Tsu insisted on leaving up year-round.

"Definitely!" Gabe was really enjoying his evening with Beverly: It was his first one out of the house since their trip to New York City. His father had grounded him immediately upon their return. Even though Milton was spending fewer hours working and was trying to be more forthcoming with Gabe and Gloria, he was still very much a dad, and Gabe was still very much in trouble.

Gabe hadn't minded too much, though—since Milton had been home more, they'd done a couple of wiring projects together and fixed the dishwasher for Gloria. Dover had even been allowed to come over during the last week, so all in all, he reflected, it could have been much worse. Also, it was actually a little bit of a relief to have a reason to come home right after school. He and Dover were celebrities now. Everyone—even Mack—had high fives for them. Dover loved the attention, but Gabe found it a little exhausting. He definitely dug the nightly break.

Beverly returned to the living room with a huge bowl of popcorn and plopped down on the couch next to Gabe. They had already gone through a bag of chips and salsa during the first movie. Now they were deep into *The Two Towers*, and all the Hobbit talk of "second breakfasts" had made them hungry again.

"So Horton's being court-martialed, huh?" She popped a kernel in her mouth.

"Yeah," Gabe said, taking a handful from the bowl, which Beverly had perched on her lap. "I guess his gray dreams can now expand to include gray prison walls," he said, crunching.

"What about Trina?" Beverly asked. "Is she back at your house?"

"No. My dad's working on reprogramming her, but she's at NSA headquarters."

"Your dad doesn't wanna take any chances on you getting a crack at her again, huh?" she joked.

Gabe laughed. "More like he doesn't want to deal with the security risk," he said. "It's pretty cool, though. Now that he's not using the basement lab as his office, we can work on projects down there. You should come over sometime," he went on. "There's some crazy stuff left over from when he was building Trina—robotics and stuff like that."

"Yeah?" Beverly said. "Do you think you could make me a robotic arm?"

On-screen, Arwen was giving Aragorn the Evenstar pendant that had hung around her neck. Gabe looked at Beverly; her skin was luminous in dim light, and her eyes were wide and bright. Yeah, she was a geek—but so was he. As Aragorn's lips sought Arwen's on-screen, Gabe closed his eyes, leaned across the popcorn bowl, and kissed Beverly. Her lips were soft and warm, and she tasted like butter and salt. Suddenly, he remembered the weird feeling he'd gotten in his stomach that day on the playground when Beverly had kissed his knee to make it better. He remembered it because he had the same feeling now.

He pulled back and looked at her. She was smiling.

"I'll build you whatever you want," he told her. "But you don't need a robotic anything. You're great just the way you are."

This time, it was Beverly who leaned in to kiss him. As his mouth met hers for the second time, he thought fleetingly of Trina—her white-blonde hair, her perfect proportions. Then, as the kiss deepened, he banished the thought from his mind. Trina was awesome, but making out with a real girl was even better.

Especially one not programmed to kill Dr. Phil.

ACKNOWLEDG-MENTS

THANK YOU VERY MUCH TO KATIE SCHWARTZ, JOELLE HOBEIKA, Lanie Davis, Sara Shandler, and the many at Alloy, past and present (especially Andy Ball for the start and Allison Heiny for the stay), who helped me; Ben Schrank at Penguin; my family and friends.